"Let me ease you into the saddle," Jack said softly, putting his hands around Claire's waist.

•

To her surprise, she saw that they were shaking. "Is something wrong?" she asked.

He didn't look at her. "I thought you might be getting stiff. You shouldn't sit too long in one position."

"Is your horse tired? I can walk, too, if—"

"No, don't worry about Thunder. He can go all night."

He looked at her then, and she saw the longing in his face. *He can go all night, and so can I,* his eyes seemed to say. *And Lord, I want to.*

Claire wondered if the moonlight exposed the flush that rose along her neck and face, or revealed the dizzying response his desire elicited in her. "You wanted to show me something," she managed to say, though suddenly she could scarcely breathe.

"Just the beauty of the land," he said, gazing up at her. "But what you've shown me is far more beautiful."

Their eyes locked. In the span of a single instant, a vivid clear image of the two of them flashed into her mind: making love on a carpet of summer wildflowers with a passion that moved the earth . . .

Bantam Books by Nancy Holder
Ask your bookseller for the titles you have missed

WINNER TAKE ALL
(*Loveswept #30*)

THE GREATEST SHOW ON EARTH
(*Loveswept #47*)

FINDERS KEEPERS
(*Loveswept #77*)

OUT OF THIS WORLD
(*Loveswept #103*)

WHAT ARE *LOVESWEPT* ROMANCES?

They are stories of true romance and touching emotion. We believe those two very important ingredients are constants in our highly sensual and very believable stories in the *LOVESWEPT* line. Our goal is to give you, the reader, stories of consistently high quality that may sometimes make you laugh, sometimes make you cry, but are always fresh and creative and contain many delightful surprises within their pages.

Most romance fans read an enormous number of books. Those they truly love, they keep. Others may be traded with friends and soon forgotten. We hope that each *LOVESWEPT* romance will be a treasure—a "keeper." We will always try to publish

LOVE STORIES YOU'LL NEVER FORGET
BY AUTHORS YOU'LL ALWAYS REMEMBER

The Editors

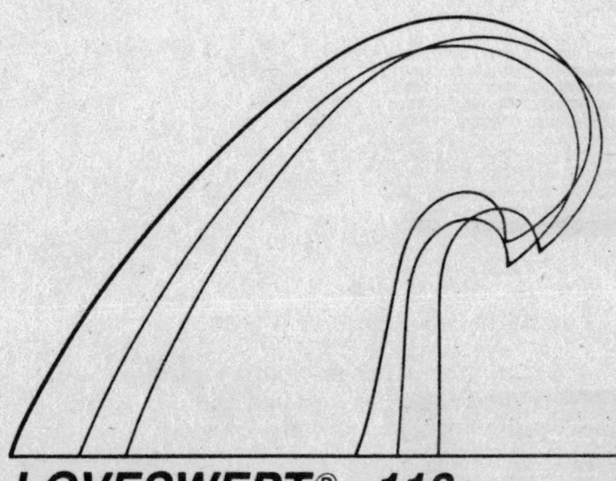

LOVESWEPT® • 118

Nancy Holder

His Fair Lady

BANTAM BOOKS
TORONTO • NEW YORK • LONDON • SYDNEY • AUCKLAND

HIS FAIR LADY

A Bantam Book / November 1985

LOVESWEPT® and the wave device are registered trademarks of Bantam Books, Inc. Registered in U.S. Patent and Trademark Office and elsewhere.

ISBN 0-553-21733-X

Published simultaneously in the United States and Canada

Bantam Books are published by Bantam Books, Inc. Its trademark, consisting of the words "Bantam Books" and the portrayal of a rooster, is Registered in U.S. Patent and Trademark Office and in other countries. Marca Registrada. Bantam Books, Inc., 666 Fifth Avenue, New York, New York 10103.

PRINTED IN THE UNITED STATES OF AMERICA

O 0 9 8 7 6 5 4 3 2 1

To my dear ones, Wayne and Leslie:

O! know, sweet love, I always write of you,
And you and love are still my argument;
So all my best is dressing old words new. . . .

—Shakespeare
Sonnet LXXVI

One

It was high dawn in Julian. The washes of lavender and mauve that streaked the sky were giving way to the warm golden glow of a cloudless Southern California morning. Planes of turquoise shone above the old-fashioned wooden buildings of Main Street: the general store; the historic Julian Hotel, built during the Gold Rush; and the antique shop on the corner that beckoned Jack Youngblood like a lighthouse as he navigated painfully down the street. His head throbbed and his eyelids seemed to be made of sandpaper. But inside the shop, comfort waited.

"Coffee," he moaned like a dying man. "Aspirin."

He walked on, cowboy boots treading the planked boardwalk, each step jarring his tender skull. The lights were on in Alcott's Antiques, and he sighed as he wrapped his right hand around the brass doorknob and let himself in.

His sister, Karen, looked up from diapering his niece and let out a low whistle.

"Good grief, Jack," she said, sliding on Megan's plastic pants and nestling her daughter against her chest. "You sure don't look like a hotshot stud."

He tried to grin at her remark, but the muscles around his mouth were too tired. He said nothing for a moment, only admired the tranquil scene of mother and child. Surrounded by copper pots and burnished pecan armoires and chairs, Karen was the picture of peaceful contentment. She was tall, like he was, dressed in jeans and a green plaid shirt that nearly matched his own, with hair the color of roasted chestnuts and eyes that were even darker. The high cheekbones and firm jaw that were rough and angular in his face were finely chiseled in hers. She was a lovely woman, and he felt a surge of brotherly affection toward her even as she teased him, rolling her eyes and tsk-tsking as he pecked her cheek.

"Just the *owner* of a hotshot stud," he corrected.

"That's not what I heard from Jessie Reynolds," she said, winking at him. "Hope you're not bent on becoming a local legend."

"Gossip later. Coffee now," he begged, his low voice even more gravelly than usual. He yawned and tickled Megan under the chin. Chubby baby fists flailed at his aquiline nose as the four-month-old squealed with delight. "Please."

Karen reached beneath the counter where the shiny brass cash register stood for the coffeepot and poured him a cup of the strong, black brew, adding three cubes of sugar. He had a sweet tooth that wouldn't quit, but in spite of all the candy and sugar he devoured, he had never had a cavity in his life. When they were kids he knew that fact had driven her crazy. Karen had been a faithful brusher, and all she had gotten for her pains was a bulk discount at the dentist's and the nickname—courtesy of her loving brother—of "Old Silver Mouth."

Right now he was Old Cotton Mouth. He licked his lips as he admired the deft way she kept Megan from grabbing the handle of the cup, and wondered if he'd ever feel coordinated again. His muscles felt as if they were made of nothing but rubber bands and wet noodles.

"You're really in a bad way, brother dear," Karen observed, placing a sympathetic hand on his shoulder as he took the coffee from her. "Poor degenerate. I'd say you outdid yourself this time."

"Just couldn't help myself."

Karen chuckled. "Yeah, I know. Listen, I've got a bottle for Megan heating in the kitchen, but I'll be right back."

"Aspirin," he pleaded.

"With some aspirin."

He gave her a grateful bob of his head, wincing when a thundercloud of pain rumbled behind his eyes. "I'll never do this again," he rasped as he took a sip of coffee.

Karen laughed airily and tousled his hair. "Oh, yes, you will. The next time Night's Fury proves out, you'll be down at the Longbranch again, buying everyone who can still stagger another round of Jack Daniel's."

"Won't."

"Will. You *will* do it all again, Jack. I'd stake a blue Delft pitcher on it. I know you." Chuckling, she disappeared around the corner.

He pursed his lips and scratched the bristles on his chin. She was right, of course. He would do a repeat performance when the occasion called for it. He was a firm believer in celebrating.

And last night he had definitely had something to celebrate. A foal sired by one of his prize stallions had been sold at auction in Dallas for a cool two million. It was a new record for his stud farm, Rancho Espejo. Now he'd raise his fees—again—and watch the horse breeders line up for the services of his horses—again. Eventually, he knew, another foal would be sold for a new record.

"And I'll celebrate again," he said, sighing, toying with the spoon in his too-hot coffee. "Youngblood," he told himself, "you've got to learn some self-control."

A flicker of blue caught his eye, and he idly glanced out the open back window that looked onto Karen's garden, which was planted to bursting with roses and pansies and hollyhocks. There was nothing unusual, only the lazy swaying of the flowers in the breeze, which brought the subtle scent of pine and floral fragrances to blend with the heady aroma of his coffee.

"Must have been a robin," he mused, glancing at the empty birdbath stationed at one end of Karen's hedge of First Love roses.

Shrugging, he lifted his cup to his mouth, then nearly poured the steaming contents into his lap as he froze with stunned surprise.

A little goatlike creature was scampering through the rose hedge, sending petals flying everywhere in a delicate pink rain.

A little goatlike creature with a single horn growing out of its forehead.

A unicorn, bending down to munch the blossoms.

Jack blinked. "This is some hangover," he mumbled. "I'm hallucinating."

A woman—no, an angel, surely, he thought—materialized from between two lattices of sweet peas and headed for the unicorn. The vision was dressed in clothes from another century: royal blue velvet slashed with silver, a wide ruff of starched lace framing an oval face, and the yellowest, shiniest hair he'd ever seen. It was as angel hair should be, wispy cascades of filigree, crowned with a circlet of wildflowers that matched the startling cobalt blue of her eyes.

"Merlin!" she called in a musical voice, and almost before the sight of her registered in Jack's bloodshot brain, the goat—the *unicorn*—bolted and the angel swooped after it, disappearing beyond his field of view.

"Karen," he whispered sorrowfully. "Karen, come quickly. I've pickled my brain."

As he rose from the stool painfully, like an old man, the angel reappeared. Only this time she was taller, and dressed in scarlet.

"Hey!" he called out, but the word was no more than a hoarse growl that startled the unicorn and sent the sprite chasing after it, muttering a panicky "Uh-oh."

Then the angel in blue darted back. Ah, there were two of them, he realized, but before he could manage another throaty growl or mournful whisper, she rushed to the window and rapped on it.

"Excuse me," she murmured, "but our unicorn is in your garden."

Staring, Jack set down his cup. "Your unicorn."

From far away she had been pretty, but up close she was enchanting, dainty as a fairy princess in her velvet dress and circlet, yet glowing with the mature beauty of a woman. The low-cut gown hugged her petite body, pushing up breasts as creamy as the ropes of pearls that lay between them. Her eyes were two huge sapphires that glanced up appealingly at him, and a rosy blush deepened her cheeks to the same hue as her small cupid's-bow lips.

"Actually it's a specially bred goat," she said in a rush. "But we call it a—"

"Claire!" another feminine voice cried from out of sight. "Ask if they have a rope or something! Oh, *no*! There's a vegetable patch!"

Not Karen's prize-winning vegetables! "Damn!" Jack swore, his head pounding, and rushed into the fray.

Claire backed away from the towering stranger as he burst through the back door of the antique shop. She was startled by the grimace on his lips and the fire in his deepset brown eyes. The screen on the window had softened and muted his otherwise haggard features.

"Claire! Claire!" her sister, Amy, called wildly. "Hurry!"

Claire looked at the man, whose tight jeans molded long, powerful legs as he ran past her and to the right of the rose hedge. His shirt sleeves were rolled to his forearms, revealing tanned flesh and big hands. Haggard maybe, she thought, but also arresting. She couldn't help but stare at him, take in the way he moved. Then, rousing herself, she gathered up her heavy skirts and petticoats and rushed after him.

"Please don't hurt Merlin," she called, stumbling over roots and trailers that the man had leaped over without noticing. One of her Chinese slippers caught in a thorn bush and she gave a cry as stickers stabbed her toes, sending sparks of pain up her leg.

From the doorway of the antique shop a woman holding a baby stepped onto the porch.

"Jack, what is it?" the woman shouted. "Do you need my shotgun?"

"No!" Claire wailed. Fear clutched her heart and she redoubled her attempts to catch up with the cowboy. Lord Petit Sirrah, their leader, had warned them about the people around here. "Above all else, ye dare not trespass," she could hear him saying. "Edgy be these country folk over their rights of ownership. Have ye a care, lest thy backside be fraught with buckshot."

"Amy, Merlin, run!" she gasped, ducking beneath a pine branch and narrowly missing another. She tried to catch her breath, but the tight lacings of her gown restricted her to shallow gulps of air. And with all the running and excitement, she was growing faint. But the vision of little Merlin being shot—perhaps *murdered* in cold blood—propelled her on.

"Please, please!" she called frantically, reaching with both hands toward the man as he disappeared around a wooden fence. "We'll pay for the damages! Please, don't—!"

"Well, I'll be damned!" the man bellowed, and Claire tripped over a rake and slammed hard against the fence. Her teeth rattled and her shoulder began to ache. Instantly the world grew dark, tilting and dimming, and she wondered if she was dreaming when she saw Merlin flash past her, a cabbage in his mouth, and the man race after him, twirling a lasso above his head.

Amy flew by, too, waving her arms, and the trio ran smack into the rose hedge in a tumble of arms and legs and unicorn horn.

A gust of petals rose like a tornado into the air, then cascaded onto the heads of man, girl, and beast. Amy was distraught, flinging her arms around Merlin's neck and shrieking, "Don't shoot! Don't shoot!" and the man was laughing so hard he was crying.

Laughing! Claire sucked in her breath.

Or tried to.

And passed out cold from the effort.

She was dimly aware that someone was touching her forehead then reaching behind to unlace the leather thongs that fastened her costume. She was conscious of tension and a low muttering, and strained to mumble a protest when the bodice of her dress was pulled down her arms, leaving her exposed in a blousy Elizabethan chemise made of tissue-thin gauze.

"She's breathing," a gravelly voice reported.

Someone was crying. Claire couldn't seem to open her eyes or speak or move. It was as if she were asleep and dreaming, but somehow she knew she wasn't. Warm, long fingers prodded gently down her spine, then swept up the back of her neck. She smelled a pungent masculine odor of leather, musk, and citrus, sensed a rush of air on her cheek and neck.

Then someone was lifting her up, enfolding her in strong, muscular arms. There was warmth all around her. Heartbeats pounded fiercely against her ear. She tried to speak and heard herself whimper, and began to float through the blackness again, falling, and then . . .

A kiss? Had someone kissed her?

* * *

"She's coming around."

Claire heard the words but couldn't place the speaker. She tried again to open her eyes and failed, lulled by the comforting darkness and the warmth of blankets tucked under her chin. She smelled wax and lemon, and, strongest of all, the sweetness of violets.

"Thank goodness," replied a deep masculine voice. "I didn't see her run into the fence, but by the look of that shoulder—"

"I'm glad you know about bones. If I'd been alone, I would've been afraid to move her. But I still wish the doctor would hurry up," said the first speaker, and Claire recognized the voice of the woman who had offered the man a gun.

And the other voice was his.

Her eyes flew open and she started to sit up, but his firm, callused hands pressed against her bare collarbones as he leaned over her, looking more haggard than ever. The woman hovered beside him, holding an open bottle of cologne and a handkerchief.

"Easy, easy," he soothed, and his tone reminded Claire of the time in Rhodesia, long ago, when her father had coaxed a lion out of the path of their Jeep. There was concern in the stranger's eyes, but insistence, too, as she obeyed the gentle pressure of the fingers molded over her flesh and leaned back against a satiny-soft pillow. They were intense eyes, almost black, with mysterious flecks of gold encircling the irises. Stallion eyes, she found herself thinking, losing herself in them. The eyes of a male animal, intent on a female . . .

She was lying in a canopy bed, sinking into a goose-down mattress with chintz hangings all around her. Then she realized with a start that beneath a sunny patchwork quilt she was wearing nothing but the see-through chemise and her tea-colored bikini panties.

He must have understood her expression of dismay, for he smiled crookedly and said, "I had to let you loose. I wasn't sure what was wrong with you, and that dress was constricting your breathing." His hands remained on her collarbones, making her tingle there, the sensations traveling over her chest and neck and creeping downward to the soft roundness of her breasts and nipples. Almost without being aware of it she drew her legs together. He was so close she could see the individual hairs on his chin and in the hollows of his cheeks, so near, she began to feel dizzy again.

"What happened to Merlin?" she asked, straining for composure. "Where's my sister?"

Amy stepped from behind the man. Her eyes were raw with crying, her long hair matted with leaves and petals, and her once-beautiful scarlet gown was muddy and torn. She looked like a grief-stricken waif, clutching the woman's baby, its pink and white face peering avidly from the frame of a fuzzy yellow blanket.

"Merlin's outside," Amy said, sitting on the edge of the bed. "Karen fed him some carrots and apples. Oh, Claire, you scared me!" Fresh tears welled in her eyes. "I thought you were dead!"

Claire smiled gently at her sister, wrapping her fingers around Amy's small wrist and giving her a squeeze. "I'm sorry. But you should know by now I'm impossible to get rid of." Her voice grew soft. "I'll never leave you, Amy."

They regarded each other lovingly, Claire seeing herself a decade younger in the girlish face of her sister. The sole difference between them lay in Amy's eyes, which were velvety chocolate. She carefully shifted the baby and returned Claire's comforting gesture. "I know."

"The doctor's on her way," the woman—Karen—put in.

"They're afraid you might have a concussion," Amy explained, biting her lower lip.

"Oh, that's silly," Claire said quickly. "I didn't hit my head." A stab of alarm made her struggle to sit up. They couldn't afford extravagances such as an unnecessary medical bill. And she was sure it was unnecessary. She'd never been sick or injured since the day their parents had passed away.

"I'm fine," she insisted.

"Like hell you are," the man said roughly. "You should see your rib cage."

"It's swollen," Amy confirmed, extracting a lock of her yellow hair from the baby's eager grasp. "He said you were going to have some terrific bruises."

Heat washed over Claire and she wished she could faint all over again. Oh, dear, she thought wretchedly, he'd seen her as good as undressed. He'd seen her rib cage and Lord knew what else—no, cancel that, she did know what else. Renaissance ladies did not wear bras—a fact the dark and compelling man must now be aware of.

And had he kissed her? Had those soft lips brushed hers for the briefest of moments? Had that tickling sensation been the scratching of his bristly beard on her chin?

"Are you all right?" the man demanded, peering at her. He frowned as he studied her face. "You just went white."

She swallowed. "We haven't been introduced," she said. "I'm Claire van Teiler."

"I told him," Amy added.

He held out a hand. "Jack Youngblood. And this is my sister, Karen, and my niece, Megan. And you're white as a damn ghost."

She managed a weak smile. "I'm very sorry about your garden."

"They won't take any money," Amy said. "I already offered."

Thank heaven, Claire thought, frowning inwardly because it bothered her to be so relieved. "But we want to repay you," she insisted, her good manners taking precedence over her good sense.

"Oh, we'll get it out of you somehow," Jack said teasingly, but she detected a note of seriousness in his voice that made her want to cover her breasts with her hands. He had seen them, of that she was sure. Had he touched them during his examination?

Had he kissed her?

"How about free tickets to the Renaissance fair?" Amy asked, her eyes shining. "Lord Petit Sirrah would let them have some, don't you think?" As if in reply, Megan blew bubbles at her, wrinkling her nose when Amy giggled and dabbed the corners of the baby's mouth with the blanket.

"Really, don't worry," Karen insisted. "No major harm was done. He ate only a few cabbages, and the roses will grow back."

The expression on Jack's face told Claire that Karen was being gracious, not honest. She and Amy—and Merlin, unfortunately—would be in Julian for a month. In that time she'd have to find some way to compensate the charming woman for Merlin's romp.

The jangle of a bell pealed in the distance.

"That'll be Doc Lewis," Karen said, and hurried out of the room.

"Really, I don't need a doctor," Claire repeated, brushing her hair away from her face. "Please, just give me back my clothes and Amy and I will be on our way."

"You'll let the doctor see you," Jack replied, giving her a stern look. He had long lashes, she noted, heavy, abundant fringes that further accentuated his intriguing eyes. Made them harder to avoid. "And then I'll drive you back to the fairgrounds."

She tossed her head and crossed her arms over her chest, remembering just in time her state of undress and catching the edge of the quilt. "Mr. Youngblood, I'm not in the habit of being ordered around, and I—"

"Claire's worried about the money," Amy cut in.

"Amy!" Claire looked at her, aghast. But her sister smiled sweetly and touched her cheek.

"Well, it's true. But this is one time you should spend something on yourself, Cunky." She turned to

Jack. "She's always buying me things and making do with the leftovers."

"Is she?" Jack asked, studying Claire. She flamed from the intensity of his gaze, sure he was reading more in her face than she cared for him to know.

The baby struggled in Amy's arms and began to cry. "Here, let me take her," Jack offered, and scooped Megan up. A warm glow lit his face as the child quieted instantly and cooed at him. A tender smile softened the sharpness of his profile and there was such love in his eyes that Claire felt her throat tighten. Cuddling the baby under his chin, he nuzzled his cheek against her dandelion hair and turned his attention back to the matter at hand.

"You'll see the doctor," he said, and started to walk out of the room.

"I will n—"

A woman carrying a black leather bag appeared in the doorway. "Whoa, Jack," she said. "You look like *you* should be my patient."

"I could use a new head," he replied, laughing. He flinched and groaned, raising the fingers of his right hand to his temple. "One with some sense in it." He gestured toward Claire. "Make absolutely sure she's in perfect condition, Jane," he told the doctor, kissing the top of Megan's head. "And send me the bill."

He was gone before Claire could voice her protest.

About a half-hour later he met them outside and nodded with satisfaction at Dr. Lewis's report that Claire was fine, just bruised and scratched. He had showered and shaved and he looked like a new man. He wore fresh jeans and a bright plaid shirt. His chestnut hair shone with highlights of gold and copper as he stationed Amy in the back of his tan pickup truck with Merlin, who was completely unrepentant of his naughtiness. The unicorn strained at the rope around his neck, eager to return to the scene of his gluttony.

"Careful, now," he ordered Claire as he wrapped his hand around her forearm and helped her into the truck's cab. There was such strength implicit in his grasp that a thrill shot up her spine. Who was this stranger, this man with a raging hangover who had nonetheless galloped to the rescue of his sister's garden and cared for a trespasser with such ferocious kindness?

And firmness, she added silently as she recalled how he had ordered her to see the doctor. She saw his forehead wrinkle with discomfort as he shut the passenger door and walked around to his side, and wished she could do something for him in return. In her mind's eye she saw herself massaging his scalp and the long column of his neck, running her hands through his hair again and again. . . .

"Are you all right?" he demanded as he climbed in beside her. "You look flushed. And you should have told me about your foot."

"You never gave me a chance," she said, inhaling his fresh scent. "Besides, they were just a few stickers."

He looked impatient. "I saw them, Claire. One of them was half an inch long."

"I have lots of calluses," she countered. "I barely felt anything."

He snorted, then started up the truck and drove down the street. As they passed the quaint buildings, men in cowboy hats waved at Jack, and women stared hard, looking to see who was sitting in the cab beside him. Claire could hear Merlin bleating in the back as if in response, and she chuckled. Despite his antics, she loved the silly animal.

Jack smiled at her quizzically. "Is something funny?"

"Not really," she replied. A man on horseback hailed the truck and Jack raised a hand in reply. "You know, this is a friendly town. I think we'll like it here."

"You will if I have anything to say about it."

Claire swallowed. "You've, uh, been very kind."

"Kind's not the word."

"About the doctor, I—I'll pay you back," she stammered, flustered by the sexy undertone of his replies. *Relax*, she told herself. *He's only flirting*.

"You already have paid me back."

She said nothing, though she could feel his gaze on her as he waited for a response. As the truck turned onto a narrow road she looked out at the passing orchards of apple trees heavy with fruit. Shades of green and peach blurred past as the pickup bounced along the blacktop.

"It seems strange to find a small town like this so close to a big city like San Diego," she murmured, almost to herself. "We all thought it would be a little more modern."

"That's not what we want here. Most of the people who live in Julian are refugees from the city and all its 'modern conveniences.'" He appraised her, indicating her elaborate costume. "Looks to me like you feel the same, only in a more extreme way."

She relaxed against the back of the seat, pleased that the conversation had grown less intimate. "I never thought of it like that exactly. But I guess you're right."

"We voted on you," he went on. "The merchants suggested that since we've made a good profit with apple festivals and fiddling contests, we might give you a try."

Give you a try. She scratched her nose. "I know. We voted on coming here too. We rarely stay anywhere as long as a month, but you have an excellent reputation."

She saw the corners of his mouth twitch. "An excellent reputation," he drawled thoughtfully. "My sister said something along those lines this morning."

They drove on in the bright, clear day. On Claire's right a huge wooden gate shut out a view of pines and manzanita, and she strained to peek around it as the truck whizzed past.

"That's my place," Jack said. "Rancho Espejo."

"Oh. I thought you worked at the antique store." As the handyman, she added silently, embarrassed that she'd judged him on his scruffy appearance.

"Nope. I'm into mating." He waited for her surprise, then grinned when he got it. "Rancho Espejo's a stud farm."

"I see," she said, and meant to ask more about it, but her eyes flew open as they came to the crest of a hill. "Look! Oh, look!"

Before them unrolled a meadow edged with fluffy pines and wildflowers. And in the center of the grassy expanse banners and shields rose above the first stages of a Tudor village made of cardboard and plaster. Two-by-fours formed lintels, and "stones" of gray canvas stretched the two-story heights of a royal fortress, staple-gunned into place and the joints covered over with planks. Farther on, Gypsy tents undulated in the breeze.

Claire clapped her hands with delight at the same time that Amy rapped on the rear window of the cab. Claire pivoted around to share her exuberance and let out an agonized gasp as her sore muscles seized and she fell forward.

"Oh, honey," Jack said, shooting out a hand to support her. Immediately he pulled the truck to the side of the road and rapped his fingers around her arms, easing her upright in a strong, protective grasp. "Are you all right?"

Abashed, she drew in her shoulders and nodded. "Sure. I just moved too fast. Really, it's nothing," she went on when he didn't let go of her. His touch soothed. As he massaged her upper arms the cramps unknotted and the pain receded. He had a magic touch, she thought, a wondrous way about him.

An unnerving way.

"I'm . . . fine."

And he had strange, gold-ringed eyes. Above

them his brows were heavy, giving him a fierce look when he set his jaw. "If it was Amy who'd been hurt, we'd be carrying her back on a palanquin."

There was no malice in his voice, but Claire's eyes flashed with defensiveness, and she retorted, "Are you insulting her?"

His answer was a tender smile, much like the one that had lit his face when he'd taken his niece in his arms. "No, Cunky. I was trying to point out that you don't treat yourself with the same care that you would her if she'd been the injured one."

Cunky. That was Amy's pet name for her, and no one else's, and it bothered her that he used it.

Yet, somehow, curiously, it sounded right on his lips. . . .

"You don't know anything about us," she said tentatively, not really wanting to sound rude but still needing to defend Amy.

He paused. "That's not exactly true. While you were unconscious Amy told Karen and me a few things."

Frowning, she asked, "Really? Such as?"

"Such as you used to live with an aunt who makes Cinderella's evil stepmother sound like a lamb."

"Oh, Amy," Claire said, sighing. It made her decidedly uncomfortable to know her sister had been spilling family secrets to this man, especially when she and Amy had made a solemn vow to put their unhappy past behind them. Amy's nightmares had only recently begun to fade, and the mere mention of Aunt Norma turned Claire's heart to ice. There was nothing to be gained in dragging memories around like heavy chains.

"And that if it hadn't been for you, Amy would still be living with her, convinced she was mentally retarded."

That much was true. Norma, with her unusual combination of outright indifference and well-targeted cruelty, had managed to twist Amy's boredom at school—caused by her superior intellect—into proof that Amy should be placed in remedial classes. It was not until Claire had taken her away to live with her that Amy had blossomed scholastically, to the point that she'd declared she'd had enough of school and had graduated with honors at sixteen.

"Well, it's not really your business," Claire said, shaking her head to clear away the old, unwanted images.

"Yes, it is." He picked up a curl of her hair and rolled it between his fingertips. "You made it my business."

Her breath caught in her throat when his knuckles caressed her cheek. His lips parted and he breathed through his nose, and she was reminded again of a great, dark horse, a charger such as a queen might tame. . . .

Did you kiss me? she pleaded silently. *Is that why I feel so drawn to you?* She licked her lips and blinked, straining to break the spell he was casting over her.

Amy knocked on the window. "Is something wrong?" she called loudly.

Claire broke free. The air in the cab crackled as she unrolled the window, and she gingerly stuck out her head. Jack's hand fell from her hair to her shoulder and rested there, burning her through the velvet.

"No, baby. Everything's fine," she assured her sister, but all at once she realized that it wasn't true. "This is our stop though," she added, reaching for the door handle.

"Easy, easy," Jack insisted, holding her arm. "Let me help you. Just hang on until I come around."

She let out a deep breath as he climbed out and ambled toward her side. Behind them Amy hopped down from the truck bed and slapped her hands against her thighs. "Hey, sweetie! Come on, lovey!" she chirruped, and Merlin threw himself into her arms. "Sir Goodwrench will be so relieved to see you all in one piece," she cooed, pulling on Merlin's beard. "Claire, we'll have to call off the search party."

"You'd better go do that," Jack cut in. "I'll take care of your sister."

"Okay," Amy agreed, missing Claire's look of entreaty as she smiled at Jack and held out her hand. "I hope we'll see each other again. I meant it about the tickets. I'll try to get them for you."

"Much obliged. I hope we'll see each other again too."

"Then we will!" she said cheerily, and darted away, staggering beneath the weight of the goat.

Claire drew herself in as he slid his hands around her waist. They were so large they nearly met at the small of her back. "I can get down by myself."

"Yes, I know." To Jack she felt as fragile as spun sugar, her waist so tiny inside the layers of clothing. "But it'll be a lot pleasanter if you let me help you. You're hurt," he added quickly, seeing the fire in her eyes.

"Okay," she said, exhaling. She clamped her hands on his wrists. Her fingers were soft yet sinewy, and he was surprised by the urgency in them. Was she frightened?

"Here we go," he said, easing her down. Other than his hands on her waist, and her hands on his, their bodies made no contact. And yet he tingled as if she had clung to him, her small, perfect breasts pressed against his chest. Body to body, flesh to flesh . . .

Heart to heart . . .

Her feet touched the ground all too soon. Then, as she stood before him on the grassy earth, he knew suddenly that his life had just changed forever. How, he did not know for certain. But no matter what happened from then on, Claire van Teiler would figure in his destiny.

No, he thought suddenly. He knew how his life had changed. He *knew*.

"Here we go," he whispered low and throatily, welcoming the journey down a new and untried path.

"What?"

Not answering, and yet answering, Jack touched her lips with his finger.

"I said, " 'Here we go,' " he repeated. "You and I, Claire. Together."

And then he kissed her.

Two

Oh, no, he was going to kiss her, Claire thought as Jack gathered her up in his arms. Even before her mind grasped what was happening, her body responded. Her heart quickened, raced. A frisson of anticipation shot through her, making her catch her breath as her spine tingled and danced. As his hands spanned the width of her back, cradling taut muscles through the velvet, her body began to catch fire, and to melt.

Oh, no—

—and when his warm lips touched hers, she was lost.

It was a kiss that froze time. The world stopped moving, then spun like a dervish as he rolled his dry lower lip over hers, nipping carefully at a corner of her mouth. He was infinitely gentle, his tenderness more overwhelming than if he had been rough and demanding. His mouth caressed her chin and the hollows of her cheeks with whisper-light, breathy strokes as soft as sighs. He pressed his lips against her forehead, her temple, the ridge of her brow. The tawny skin of his face brushed her jaw as he held her carefully, as if she might break in a more passionate embrace. Her lids flickered and closed. The last things she saw were his heavy lashes and the wrinkles in his forehead, telling her that for him, too, this was something all-encompassing, something to which he was giving himself without hesitation.

"Ah," he whispered. "Claire."

Her ears roared with her own name. She was filled with him. Everything smelled like fresh soap and spice, and felt like smooth, firm flesh, and her feminine spirit was generous and wanting and new. Her soul reached for his. She heard herself gasping, heard his answering moan. Her loins quickened and the tips of her breasts began to contract with sensation.

Then, suddenly, her soul plummeted back to earth. What was she doing? She gave a muffled protest and struggled in his embrace. At once he released her and she took a step backward, covering her heaving breasts with a trembling hand.

"Did I hurt you?" Jack asked, bending down to peer anxiously into her face. "I forgot myself. Your shoulder—"

She was appalled. Why had she permitted it? Why had she *encouraged* it?

She stared at him. Why had she yielded to him? How had he elicited such a reaction from her? It always took her a long time to let people near her, and yet this man had penetrated her ivory tower of reserve as if there had been no walls at all.

"Claire?" he asked, alarmed. "Did I hurt you?"

She continued to stare, not really seeing his commanding physical beauty. Instead, she felt it. Her body burned as if his hands still touched her, moved, explored, as if his lips still stroked and caressed her mouth. She shook slightly, unable to escape the afterimages of desire.

Slowly the events of the previous hours dropped onto her shoulders: an endless drive from the last Renaissance fair in Phoenix, a flat tire in the desert, the search for Merlin, the accident.

The kiss.

The abandon, the giving, the joining.

It was too much for her. She couldn't cope with what he had awakened in her, not with all the other uncertainties she carried. To her horror a single tear pooled in the corner of her eye and slid down her cheek.

"No," she said. "No, you didn't . . . hurt . . . me." She wiped the tear away and turned on her heel, the rich blue fabric of her dress flaring behind her like a train.

"Don't go," he called after her. "Don't run."

"You didn't hurt me!" Her voice cracked.

"Then who did?"

She pretended not to hear as she put more distance between them. She gritted her teeth as needles of pain pricked her sore foot.

"Who did, Lady Claire?"

" 'Look how fair my lord doth smile,
How fair his looks and words do seem.
Oh, to be a lady fine
and wear his heart upon my sleeve.' "

Claire put down her lute and stared into the communal campfire, which the fire marshal of Julian had permitted the Gypsy nomads to build in the center of their compound. Around her the other members of the Renaissance troupe—nearly a hundred strong—quietly applauded her ballad. The flames flickered on their smiling faces, and Claire felt protected and safe in their company.

The group journeyed year-round, moving in their trailers and vans to prearranged locations, where they erected their old English village for a few days or a week. Besides offering crafts and food booths, the troupe performed dances and sang ballads, ending each day at dusk with a merry maypole dance before Their Royal Highnesses, the King and Queen of the May. Clad in elaborate ruffs, hats, and stomachers, speaking Elizabethan English, each member strove to add a strand to the magical tapestry of other times, other lands. In Claire's opinion they succeeded admirably. To her it was like living in a dream.

She and Amy had traveled with the fair for a full summer, their first taste of freedom. The first of many together, without anyone to answer to, without fear.

"Cunky. He shouldn't have called me that," she muttered, absently gliding her fingers across the four strings of the lute.

"Did you say something?" Amy asked. She and Claire were dressed identically in jeans and billowing muslin shirts with flowing sleeves and lace at the wrists like the garments of eighteenth-century highwaymen. Shawls woven in the muddy blues and greens of the Campbell tartan were threaded through their arms. Amy, sewing a miniature doublet for Lord Petit Sirrah, who was a midget, had secured her golden hair with a headband of silver braid. Claire's hair streamed over her shoulders as she picked up a stick and rubbed it on the granite stones of the campfire, sighing to herself.

"I was just thinking," Claire replied, feeling silly. For heaven's sake, she'd been on her own since she was eighteen, and taking care of a child too. Why on earth was she acting like an infatuated teenager?

"Thinking's dangerous, Cunky," Amy teased. "Better watch it."

Cunky again. Claire fed the stick into the fire. "I think I'll go to bed," she said glumly. "I'm tired."

"Is your shoulder stiff?" Amy queried, concern filling her eyes.

"No. I'm okay."

As she stood, Petit Sirrah raised his coffee cup to her. There were bread crumbs in his beard, and with his curly red hair, he looked like a leprechaun. " 'Tis right cheerful I be, wench, that ye be not injured. Careful must ye be around these country folk!"

Claire smiled and shook her head. Unlike the rest of the troupe, Lord P. S. never dropped his fantasy alter-ego. She often wondered if it had to do with his being a midget, or if he was merely an eccentric. He fashioned himself a mystic and a dreamer, and he was certain he was a reincarnation of Monarcho, Queen Elizabeth I's favorite jester. There were times when Claire and Amy believed it too.

"It was my own fault," she reminded him. "I was chasing after Merlin and I ran into a fence."

"Aye, so ye have said. But I would like to know, who be that young lord chasing after ye? No use to protest, lass, we all have seen ye kissing."

Amy looked at her with faint shock. Picking up her lute, Claire shrugged and said nothing, though inwardly her entire body was blushing.

"His name! Give us his name!" Petit Sirrah called, chortling.

"We weren't kissing," Claire said. Everyone tittered. "I had something in my eye."

"Aye, stars," Petit Sirrah shot back, and some of the others laughed aloud.

"You guys have dirty minds," Amy said loyally, laying a strip of gold braid down the center of the doublet and appraising it critically.

"There be nothing dirty about kissing," Petit Sirrah replied, discovering the crumbs in his beard and brushing them out. "Though I'll warrant your sister doth not believe it."

"I'll say good night again," Claire cut in, waving her finger at him. "And keep your warrants to yourself, milord."

" 'Tis your problem, Mistress Claire, that *ye* keep to *thyself* too much."

"*I* don't think so." Amy smiled sweetly at her sister. In the firelight her hair glittered and her skin was rosy, but Claire remembered that small face tight with worry when they'd been forced to live with Aunt Norma.

Claire could still see herself standing in the foyer of Norma's dreary old house in Michigan, her books in a heap around her feet as Amy clung to her, sobbing, "Cunky, don't go away to school! Don't leave me with Auntie!" And Norma, standing on the stairs, tight-lipped and merciless, snapping, "I don't know why I bother. I should send you both to an orphanage."

The difference between Amy's appearance then and now cheered Claire. She was overreacting, she told herself. She was just tired. That was why the stranger affected her so much. She was making, in the words of a fellow Renaissance person, "much ado about nothing."

She smiled back at Amy. "Good night, baby," she said, and headed for the minivan that was their home.

The night breeze billowed with the scent of grass and honeysuckle, and Claire breathed it in as she opened the door of the van. Heavier smells permeated the interior—heather and dried rose and jasmine, blended into the potpourri that they used to stuff the sachets and embroidered pillows they sold in their fair booth.

Claire hesitated in the doorway, and smelled again fresh soap and the musk of maleness. She closed her eyes against the tantalizing memory of Jack Youngblood's kiss. There had been nothing like it in her life. He had branded her with it, eliciting a sensuality within her that she had never known she possessed. Even now it made her tremble.

She should tell Amy, she thought. There were no secrets between them. But this was so intensely private, she knew she couldn't tell even her sister, the one person in the world she wholeheartedly trusted.

Then a cry rose up, and a cheering, and Claire heard the sound of approaching hoofbeats.

"Lady Claire!" Petit Sirrah warbled. " 'Tis your swain!"

Claire looked past the campfire to the silhouettes of the pines, and she saw him there, galloping toward the group on a huge ebony horse. *Youngblood, in your blood, Youngblood, in your blood*, the horse's hooves tattooed against the earth. *In your blood, in your blood—*

"God gi'good den," Petit Sirrah hailed as Jack approached. He stood and swept a courtier's bow. "Welcome to our humble village, milord."

Claire heard the amusement in Jack's tone as he touched the brim of his cowboy hat and said, "Much obliged." He clicked his teeth at the horse, then brought it up short and leaned over the pommel.

"Hi, Amy. How are you tonight?"

"Couldn't be better." Her voice was light and silvery, untroubled. Her sister was like a piece of crystal, Claire thought, filled with light and empty of shadow.

And the man on the horse, to Claire, was nothing but shadow. His mystery and intimidating looks reflected off Amy without affecting her, but Claire stood in the long stretch of his towering outline, watching.

Waiting.

"Let me introduce you to everybody," Amy chirped, jumping to her feet. She laughed merrily. "Well, there's a whole bunch of us, so maybe I'll just work on a few at a time. Let's see." She glanced around at the circle of faces. "You should meet Their Highnesses, of course. This is Commander Andrew Cunningham and his wife, Hazel."

Claire couldn't help a smile as the elderly couple beamed at Jack, and Commander Cunningham stopped drawing on his pipe to offer his hand. "I'm Unites States Navy, retired," he explained. "The missus and I joined up two years ago—"

"Three," Hazel corrected him pleasantly.

"Three," the commander agreed. "Started out as rank peasants and worked our way up to royalty."

"Andrew was bored," Hazel explained. She looked at him adoringly. "We always wanted to travel."

"Bought us a Winnebago, and here we are. Good crew." He bobbed his head in Petit Sirrah's direction, who acknowledged it with an expression of utter noblesse oblige.

"And this is Keith and Susan Mandell." Amy pointed out her and Claire's closest friends, who were dressed in jeans and beads like sixties flower children, complete with matching black hair that trailed to the smalls of their backs.

"Hey," Keith said, smiling.

"They're into stained glass," Amy explained. "They sell year-round this way."

Jack was gracious as he met each new person, but Claire saw that he was distracted, forever searching the sea of faces beyond the orange cast of the fire.

Looking for me, she thought, and wondered if she escaped inside the van would he have the nerve to demand entry. He was certainly capable of it. Somehow she knew he was used to getting what he wanted.

So she stood, waiting for him, drawing in a ragged breath of awe as the moonlight shimmered around him. He sat on his horse like a conquering warrior, his hat a crusader's helmet, his suede jacket a leather breastplate.

Then, without any prompting, he turned and looked directly at her. Without a signal from him the horse ambled toward her.

He drew the huge animal alongside, his boot even with her shoulder, and touched the brim of his hat again.

"God gi' good den," he drawled, eyes twinkling.

" 'Tis a good den," she replied.

"Whatever that means. I thought you might like to go riding."

She arched her brows. "Well, we have to work on some costumes early in the morning and then in the afternoon I was planning to practice—"

"Not tomorrow. Now."

"But you have only one horse," she blurted out without thinking.

He was wearing gloves; they reminded her of gauntlets. "I thought we'd better double, seeing as how your shoulder's strained."

Amy was observing from the campfire. When Claire glanced at her she waved and returned to her sewing.

"No, thank you," Claire said. "I was just getting something for my sister. We have a lot of work to do before the fair opens and—"

"I won't take no for an answer." The moon passed behind a cloud, shrouding him in a sudden wash of darkness, yet Claire could still see the gleam in his eyes. He paused as if waiting for her to speak, and when she didn't, he added, "After all, you owe me something for ruining my garden."

"Y-your *sister's* garden."

"And *your* doctor bill." He chuckled low in his throat. "We'll call it square if you take a ride with me. I won't keep you long, say, an hour or so."

"We'll pay you back," she said primly, drawing herself up. "Amy and I—"

"I like that blouse on you." His gaze swept up and down in a practiced, though appreciative judgment. This must be the way he evaluates his mares, she thought self-consciously, wondering what he saw, how he saw her.

"I liked the other one better," he went on, and when she flushed scarlet, he swung off his horse, laughing, and put his hand on her arm.

The moment he touched her she stiffened. His laughter turned to a rueful, contrite smile that softened his features. "I'm sorry. That was out of line. Please, Lady Claire, ride with me. The night's still and the moon is out, and I want to show you something beautiful."

Youngblood, in your blood, love in your blood, love . . .

Something beautiful.

She shook her head. "No, I can't possibly."

"We'll just ride," he promised. "Nothing else. After all, ma'am, I'm a cowboy, and we cowboys are a chivalrous breed. May I get lost in the desert without a canteen if I try any funny stuff."

She had to smile. He must have taken it for assent, because he wrapped his arms around her waist and lifted her onto the horse in a fluid motion before she could say a word. Just as easily he mounted in front of her and clasped her arms around his waist, patting them with his left hand as he took up the reins with the right. The crowd around the campfire cheered, and Claire steadfastly ignored them.

"Are you all right? No pain?"

"No."

"Let me know if you get uncomfortable."

I already am, she wanted to say. *I'm so uncomfortable with you that I—*

"Care for a jellybean?" he asked as he clucked to the horse. "There're some in my jacket pocket."

"No thank you." It was an offbeat, pleasant thing for him to say, and it helped her feel more at ease. But with her arms around him she was on guard, terribly aware of each undulation of muscle in his abdomen as he swayed with the rhythm of the horse. His stomach was hard and tight and she tried to move her hands without seeming obvious. Bending forward, he patted the horse and spoke to it, and his jacket stretched across broad shoulders. She drank in each detail, fascinated.

"Here, baby," he said, and she started. He reached into his pocket and drew out a handful of jellybeans.

Then he laughed as he rocked forward in the saddle and fed them to the horse. "Two of a kind, eh, sugar?" He popped a couple into his own mouth and chewed with relish. He grinned at Claire. "Neither one of us has any self-control."

"Whither goest thou?" Lord Petit Sirrah called. "Art hieing away with our sweet Claire?"

"I guess you could say that," Jack called back. Beneath his breath he added, "But I sure couldn't." Claire couldn't help a chuckle.

"Watch it back there," he said in a theatrical whisper. "No making fun of the locals."

"Cunky, where are you going?" Amy asked, rising and dancing toward them. The horse nickered at her and she held out a tentative palm, laughing when the horse nosed it. "Oh, it tickles! What a beautiful horse! Is it a boy or—" She ducked down for a moment, then looked up at Jack. "It's a boy," she announced.

"Very much so," Jack replied.

"I'll say." Amy flashed the man a saucy grin.

Claire closed her eyes. "Amy," she said warningly. "Don't be crude."

"Well, I was just curious," Amy retorted.

"I'm taking your sister to see the land around here," Jack told Amy. "Is that all right?"

"Sure," Amy said without hesitation. "Could I go too sometime?"

"Tomorrow if you want."

"Wow. Thanks." She smiled up at Claire. "Have fun. I'll sleep on the other side so you won't have to crawl over me when you get back."

"That's sweet," Claire said, mildly annoyed that Amy was taking this semi-abduction with such lack of concern. After all, the two of them were rarely separated. Didn't it bother her in the least that her sister was galloping off with a complete stranger?

"What's your horse's name?" Amy ran a hand along the stallion's neck. "He's so shiny."

"Thunder. I brush him a lot."

"When you're not chasing unicorns," Amy shot back, giggling.

"Or Botticelli angels," he rejoined.

"What are those?" she asked, her oval face round with innocence. "Claire, is he making a joke?"

"I don't know," Claire answered.

Jack said, "Giddap," and Amy capered backward as the horse began to move. She waved and Claire waved back, and then Jack turned the horse toward the thicket of trees.

"Of course I wasn't joking," he said as the pungent odor of the pines enveloped them in the darkness. Above them an owl hooted and there was a rush of wings against the full yellow moon. Claire tilted back her head and saw a vast sea of stars flowing among the inlets of branches and twigs.

Jack fell silent, occasionally reaching into his pocket for a jellybean. Shadow and light ebbed and flowed across his jaw as he chewed, and the breeze rippled his wavy hair at the nape of his neck. He was beautiful enough to be an angel himself, she mused, flushing belatedly at his compliment.

A wild thrill of panic washed through her. What was she doing there? she thought nervously. Why had she come with him?

"Have you been on horseback before?" Jack asked, perhaps sensing her rising anxiety.

"Lots of times," she told him. "I had my own horse once, for a season."

"Oh? Where?"

"In Argentina," she began, then trailed off. She didn't want to talk about herself. How wary she was, she thought sadly, contrasting her behavior with Amy's.

He laughed his low, sexy laugh. "What on earth were you doing there? Somehow I'd thought you hadn't done much traveling. Your aunt didn't sound like the type."

"She wasn't. But my parents were photojournalists," she said. "They took me everywhere."

"What a great childhood. We mostly stayed on my parents' ranch, punching cows and shearing sheep." He stretched slightly, straightening his back, calling her attention to the breadth of it.

"Yes, it was great," she said softly. "I wish Amy could have had—"

Suddenly the horse stopped. Jack touched Claire's hand and whispered, "Look. By that rock."

Stock-still, a tiny fawn trembled beside a granite boulder, its liquid eyes wide with fear as it stared at the intruders. It cowered beside the rock, its slender legs and tiny feet useless in their terror-induced paralysis. Its reddish-brown flanks shook. The moonlight beamed down on it like a searchlight, and the creature stared unseeing in the brightness, its gaze riveted to Claire's.

Then the horse stamped its foot and the little fawn bolted and leaped into the forest, white tail flashing once before the trees concealed it.

"I'm surprised we caught it unawares," Jack said. "It's probably an orphan."

"Oh, poor thing," Claire said. "Poor baby."

Jack gave her hand a squeeze. "It'll be all right. The deer around here are so tame, they walk right into our yards and nose in the trash cans. It'll get plenty to eat. Maybe some kid will even adopt it." He kept his gloved fingers wrapped around hers, ducking to avoid a tree branch, tapping Thunder's sides with his boot heels. The horse moved on.

"Now, you were telling me about your folks," he said. "They're journalists?"

She took a breath, wishing they would talk about something else. Yet somehow she felt compelled to answer his questions, to allow him into her privacy yet further.

"My parents died in a rafting accident when I was thirteen. Then Amy and I went to live with my father's sister."

"Aunt Norma."

"Yes."

He was quiet for a moment. Then he lifted her hand to his cheek and molded it against her palm. "Poor baby," he whispered. "Oh, poor, sweet thing."

For an instant she thought he was mocking her, using the exact words she'd spoken when she'd pitied the fawn, but just as quickly she realized that he was sincerely sorry.

"It's okay," she said, touched and embarrassed by his sympathy. "It happened almost fourteen years ago. More than half my lifetime."

Without speaking he took off his glove and ran his bare fingertips over the back of her hand. She swallowed at the electricity of skin on skin. Then he laced his fingers through hers and brought her hand against his heart.

His voice was husky with compassion. "And was it very bad?"

"It was wonderful when I was little," she said, changing the subject. "My parents were such fascinating people! We were never in the same place for more than a few weeks. My mom tutored me. I used to be able to speak Swahili," she added proudly. "As well as some French and German, and I still remember my Spanish. We were very big on South America."

"And then they passed on?" Jack asked.

She sighed. "Oh, no, we had two years after Amy was born. She was premature and Mom nearly lost her. I think we were in Bangkok at the time. Anyway, my parents decided it was time for them to 'become responsible adults,' as they were fond of saying."

She chuckled wistfully. "They weren't very good at it though. They were awfully flighty. They almost forgot Amy's first Christmas! If I hadn't reminded them, they would've jetted off to Australia to do a story on the Great Barrier Reef!"

"I see." His voice sounded gruff. "But you remembered Christmas—for Amy."

She shifted, not understanding the undercurrent of tension—or was it anger?—in his voice.

"Yes. I didn't want her to have to spend it with just me and Aunt Norma. After Amy was born, they'd leave us with Norma whenever they traveled," she explained.

"And are the two of you running away from Norma now?"

Claire frowned. "No. As a matter of fact, I happen to be Amy's legal guardian, and I have been since I was twenty-one. Is that all right?"

"Hey," he said, pressing her hand against his

chest. She tried to ignore the deep, stable beating of his heart, warm and vibrant beneath his jacket. "Don't take offense. I'm just curious about you."

"You sound like you're judging us. Amy finished school early and we went on the road, just like we'd always planned. I'm going to show her the way it was for me when I was little. She grew up on stories about our adventures. There was nothing back in Michigan for us."

"I'm not judging you."

"And besides, it really isn't your business."

"Oh, yes, it is," he countered confidentially. "You know it is." He squeezed her hand. "The bond between you two is so strong I can feel it, just like my heartbeat. It intrigues me. I thought my sister and I were close, but you and Amy . . ." Turning her wrist, he kissed her palm. "Claire, I want to be that close to you."

She swallowed. She hadn't expected him to say that. "I want to go back."

He didn't speak for a long time. He stopped Thunder and they sat beneath the stars and the pines. His body warmth poured into her and she had to fight not to close her eyes and lean her cheek against his broad back.

"It's too late to go back," Jack said. "For both of us."

Then he tugged on the reins and the horse walked on, deeper into the forest.

They rode on in the night. Claire lost track of time. Hours or minutes or years could have passed in the enchanted solitude. It was as if they'd roamed the earth together forever, traveling through the evergreen forest, the soft clomping of the horse's hooves punctuated with an occasional owl hoot or a scurrying in the underbrush.

After Claire's hesitant explanation about her past they had spoken perhaps a dozen more sentences, and then the words—or the need for them—ceased. But the silence between them was not awkward.

For Claire it was filled with wonder and confusion.

And for Jack it was the same.

I like him, Claire admitted. *I trust him. But why does that make me sad?*

I want her, Jack thought. *I want her in my life always. But why? I like her, but I like all the women I've been involved with. I respect them, too, as I respect her. I want . . .*

What? What did he want?

Neither spoke these thoughts aloud. Neither told the other what was blossoming in their hearts. And yet, like the warmth of their bodies, the feelings and emotions surged from one to the other, passing into their blood, mingling and changing and returning in new shades and intensities. Above them the sky was blue-black and full of stars, like handfuls of brilliants flung from a lady's silk purse onto a blanket of velvet. The light gleamed down on Claire's yellow hair and Jack's felt hat, and seemed to glow around their silhouettes, so strong was the force that was building between them. Their veins sang with the fullness of it.

It was the force of love.

Without speaking Jack stopped Thunder and dismounted, swinging his right leg over the stallion's head and sliding off.

"Let me ease you into the saddle," he said, reaching up to put his hands around her waist. To her surprise she saw that they were shaking.

"Is something wrong?" she asked.

He didn't look at her. "I thought your shoulder might be getting stiff. You shouldn't sit too long in one position."

"Is your horse tired? I can walk, too, if—"

"No, you ride. You've had a long day. And don't

worry about Thunder. He's a strong animal. He can go all night."

He looked at her then, and she saw the raw longing in his face. *He can go all night, and so can I,* his eyes seemed to say. *And Lord, I want to.*

She wondered if the moonlight exposed the flush that rose along her neck and face or revealed the dizzying response his desire elicited in her. As he touched her, helping her shift her weight into the cradle of the saddle, her body alternately froze and burned. Her thighs tensed and her stinging breasts swelled inside the lacy confines of her bra. She was conscious of the firm, smooth leather beneath her and the musky odor of the stallion. But most of all she was aware of Jack's trembling hands as they gripped and held her.

"You—you wanted to show me something," she managed to say, though suddenly she could scarcely breathe.

He gazed up at her. "Just the beauty of the land," he said. "But what you've shown me is far more beautiful."

Their eyes locked. In the span of a single instant a vivid, clear image of the two of them flashed into her mind: nude, making love on a carpet of summer wildflowers with a frenzy that moved the earth. She saw the ripple of muscles on his abdomen, the power in his legs, the mat of dark brown hair on his chest. She saw him lying above her, her breasts pressing against his heaving chest. Everything was so real, she believed she was seeing the future—their future. With a gasp she tore her gaze away and whispered, "Jack, I can't. Please."

He put his hand on her thigh. He knew what she'd been thinking as surely as if she'd told him. Telepathy had flashed something between them, if not thoughts exactly, then emotions and yearnings. He could sense her heart nearing his, her visions of him, her desires.

"Why not, Claire? It's what we both want," he said softly.

She smiled nervously. "Would you laugh if I told you I'm not that kind of girl?" Before he could answer she hurried on. "Besides, what would Amy think?"

"Amy's not here. She doesn't have to know."

"She'd know. We're so close." Experimentally she touched her heels to Thunder's flanks. The horse took a few steps forward, breaking contact with Jack.

"Why do you care if Amy knows?" he persisted, striding to catch up with her as the horse ambled on.

"She's only sixteen. I should set a good example."

"Being such a paragon must put a damper on your social life." He touched Thunder's muzzle and the horse immediately stopped.

"I don't include jumping into bed with strange men in my definition of social life," she retorted.

"And I'll bet there wasn't much time for boyfriends when you were raising her," he went on. "And I sure as hell bet Aunt Norma wasn't keen on the idea of dating."

"It was a small price to pay."

"But you don't need to go on paying it. You're not in perpetual debt." He climbed onto a boulder, bringing his head even with her shoulders. "Come to me, Lady Claire."

Placing a hand on the back of her neck, he eased her face toward his. His lips were incredibly soft, his kiss insistent but gentle. In the black night a crow cawed as Claire closed her eyes, melting into the kiss, losing herself. She felt herself turning into a star, glowing and brilliant, shining for the man who now put his other hand around her waist and began to take her out of the saddle.

Something moved in the forest. It startled Claire and broke the spell.

"No," she said, gasping. "We mustn't." She eased the horse back. Thunder complied, dancing away from Jack. "I don't want you to love me."

"Yes, you do." He came toward her again, reaching for Thunder's bridle.

"I want you to take me back to the camp," she insisted, running a hand through her hair. The moonlight glittered on it, making it seem as if it were made of silver.

"Claire—"

"Will you take me back?"

"Claire, please, you don't understand. What I feel—it's new to me—but it's more than I ever—"

She flicked the reins and turned the stallion around. Obediently Thunder began to lope toward the forest.

"Dammit!" Jack bellowed. "You come back here! You can't run away for the rest of your life! Claire!"

"I can do anything I want!" she shouted over her shoulder.

"Then come back here!"

"I don't want to!"

"Oh, yes, you do!"

He watched her disappear into the forest. "Youngblood, you have got to learn some self-control," he admonished himself, and began the trek home.

Fifteen minutes later he pushed a pine branch out of his way and found Claire on the other side of it, waiting for him.

She blushed furiously. "I couldn't just leave you out there. After all, this is your horse."

He put two fingers to his hat, both amused and touched by her blush. "What's mine is yours," he replied. Silently he added, *Including my heart. And before this month is up, Lady Claire,* I'll *have* your *heart too.*

Three

Jack led Thunder while Claire rode the towering creature. Though the stallion knew the way by heart, his master prodded him to be careful of the paths he chose, for he carried precious cargo.

Jack caught Claire yawning and thought of the long day she'd had. Then he grinned. He himself had been up for over forty hours—and a good number of them had been spent in earnest, toll-taking celebration. How long ago that all seemed now, as if it had happened to him in another lifetime.

And how odd, to think of having made love so recently to Jessie Reynolds, a woman who liked him but didn't love him, and who was glad that the feeling was mutual.

A thrill shot through Jack as he studied the fairy princess who had alighted so near. *I've never slept with someone I truly loved,* he realized with lightning clarity. *I've been just like one of my studs—mating to slake my thirst, but with no true, deep feeling within me.*

But Lord, how can I think I love her? I don't even know her.

A voice inside his mind answered: *Oh, yes, you do, Jack Youngblood. Yes, you do.*

"Look, the dawn is breaking," Claire said, interrupting his reverie. "We stayed out all night! Amy will be worried."

The moon was low on the horizon and the stars were dim. Flares of lavender and orange rippled across the midnight sky like banderoles of silk, the heralds of the morn.

"Amy will be asleep," Jack replied gently.

They cleared the forest and entered the encampment. Last night's bonfire was nothing but ash. The campers and vans and Their Majesties' Winnebago—the Royal Standard staked into the ground by the front door, flapping in the morning breeze—were shut tight and quiet. Birdsong was the only sound in the air. Beyond the modern means of transportation, the picturesque English village rose like an anachronistic mirage in the center of the meadow. More work had been done on it since Jack had last seen it, and he marveled at the inventiveness of this pack of Gypsies. Paper looked like wood, and wood like stone.

Still, to him it was nothing but a fantastic effort to transform reality into escape. He wasn't sure if he approved of such a fairy-tale sort of life. For him living meant tilling the earth, honest work, family. Castles made of plaster were too insubstantial to base one's existence around them.

To base *her* existence around them.

He brought himself back to the moment, to find Claire straining to dismount while at the same time protecting her sore shoulder. He moved to help, but she kicked her boot out of the stirrup and trailed down the side of the horse with an ethereal grace that made his chest tighten. Her shawl loosened from around her shoulders. Beneath it the filmy blouse clung to her slight frame, then billowed as she stepped away from Thunder and gave the horse a pat.

"I didn't realize we'd been gone so long." She yawned again, covering her mouth with her small hand. "You said we'd ride for an hour."

He chuckled. "The time got away from me. I think the world sped up while we were in the forest."

"Yes, it seems that way to me too." She looked at him wonderingly. Then her blue eyes darkened and her expression grew wary. "I have to go."

"She's asleep, big sister." He touched her hair, enjoying the baby-fine texture. When her lids flickered in response his heart rejoiced. Since he had vowed to win her, each moment they were together seemed a priceless treasure, not to be squandered. He mustn't waste the gift of time. Time was his enemy and his friend, to be used wisely in the quest for the hand of the Lady Claire. . . .

"I have to go," she said again, and then, in a low, wistful voice she added, "In a month I'll be gone."

Maybe not, he said inwardly. *I pray not.*

"I'll come by later to take you and Amy to see my spread." He stroked her earlobe with his little finger as he combed her curls. "You'd better get some sleep now. You look tired."

She smiled weakly, obviously ignoring his caress. "I must look terrible."

"Never." He stopped smiling. "I'll come for you, Claire. Until then, sleep well."

She shook her head. "We have too much to do to get ready for the fair. Costumes to sew, sachets to fill—"

"It'll all get taken care of. A few hours won't change anything." He cocked his chin. "I guess that's not true, is it? A few hours have changed everything."

Her eyes grew wide. The stars have fallen into them, Jack thought, caught by their striking color. Was she really made of flesh and blood? Or was she just a vision spun from dreams, like the rest of her world?

"Nothing has changed for me," she said seriously. "Jack, my place is here. With Amy."

Her place was here indeed. With him. "And if there were no Amy?"

She crossed her arms over her chest. "There is, though. And you don't know what it was like for her. I had my parents. They took me all over the world, loved me, cared for me. They died when Amy was only two. She hardly remembers them. Norma detested both of us. I was the only one there for my sister."

"Other people need you too." His voice took on a gravelly roughness that he regretted. His impatience would frighten her away, of that he was sure. If he reached out too quickly, she'd dart away, never to return.

"I give what I can."

"You have a lot of love inside you, Claire. Enough for Amy and . . . others."

"I give what I can," she repeated steadfastly.

He looked at her hard, saw the color rise in her cheeks. She was struggling with herself not to say—or do—more. Damn, if only he could read her the way he read horses, he thought. If only he knew the right words, the right actions.

But he sensed this was the time to back off. She was exhausted, and he was new to her. She had put her sister first for so long that it was a reflex.

His sigh was heavy as he nodded. "All right, Cunky. We'll do it your way."

He put his foot in the stirrup and prepared to swing himself into the saddle. Just before he did, Claire brushed past him. He felt a satin sigh against the corner of his mouth, and he touched his lips as he turned to look at her retreating back.

Had she kissed him? he wondered. Was that a kiss?

I give what I can, he heard her sweet voice saying.

"Oh, yes, please do," he whispered after her. "Please, my lady fair."

Though Claire was careful when she crept into the van, Amy stirred and mumbled, "That you, Cunk?"

Amy was wearing a white nightgown with a ruffle under her neck. She'd fallen asleep reading a book.

There were three more fanned beside her, none of which Claire recognized in the muted darkness. She was trying to make out one of the titles when Amy gathered them up and thrust them into an opened trunk beside the bed.

Yawning, she shut the lid and lay back against a pile of velvet pillows. To Claire she looked incredibly young.

Amy chuckled. "Wow, that was some ride. You've been gone all night. He sure is cute."

"I'm sorry. I hope you didn't worry."

"Merlin escaped again," Amy told her, turning over. "Lord P. S. chased him into the pine trees and got attacked by a deer."

"Oh, no! Is he hurt?"

"No. He scrambled up a tree. He looked so funny, shaking his fist and swearing. 'Zounds!' " she cried, imitating him. "The deer was just protecting her fawn. No big excitement." She slid a sly glance at Claire. "Nothing like *your* evening."

"We just went riding," Claire said defensively.

"On one horse. Get something in your eye again?"

"Amy, it wasn't any big deal. Jack doesn't mean anything to me."

"Then why are you turning red?"

Claire pulled her blouse over her head and reached for the hooks on her bra. "Honestly, Amy. Nothing happened!"

Amy shrugged. "Honestly, Claire. You're twenty-six. Maybe something should."

"I'm shocked! Is that how I brought you up?"

"Cunky-pie, we're living in the twentieth century," Amy said, then giggled. "Well, most of the time anyway. You and I spend half our lives in the sixteenth century. But I do know about the birds and the bees. I mean, after all, you taught me about them."

Claire unzipped her jeans and slithered them

down her legs. "I also taught you about the difference between sex and love, I hope."

Claire picked up a pale pink gown and pulled it over her head, smoothing it down. She thought of Jack's hands and suppressed a tingle of desire, busying herself with folding her jeans and draping them over the edge of a box of ribbons.

"Claire, if you . . . messed around, I'm not shocked," Amy assured her. "I know women get natural urges the same as men."

Claire's mouth dropped open. "After all," Amy continued, "when will you ever have time to fall in love with somebody? We're on the road all the time. Once in a while you'll want—"

"Amy Mildred van Teiler!" Claire cried. "Is this what you really believe? What about you? Are you—do you—"

"Of course not!" Amy retorted indignantly. "I mean, I haven't found anybody I want to do it with. The first time should be really special."

"*Every time* should be really special." Claire sank onto the bed. "Oh, dear, I've failed you somewhere if this is how you think."

Amy laid a comforting hand on Claire's back. "Cunk, when I graduated from Revelle High last year, over half my girlfriends were sleeping with their boyfriends. Times have changed."

"Then I don't like these times."

Amy rubbed Claire's neck. "Don't tell me *you're* a virgin!"

Claire pursed her lips. The incredulity in Amy's voice made her feel like an old maid.

"You can't be!"

"Amy . . ."

"You're not," Amy said, triumph welling into a titter. "I can tell by the look on your face. You never were much good at hiding how you feel. Lucky for you we aren't traveling gamblers. We'd go broke in a week."

"Humph."

It was true. Claire wasn't a virgin, but she was the closest thing to one. Always living in the shadow of Aunt Norma, she had lived a circumspect life to say the least. She was terrified that Norma would make good on one of her many threats to take Amy away from her.

Then, when Claire had staved off that potential calamity by becoming Amy's legal guardian, Amy had only been eleven—an impressionable age, Claire knew, when her sister would be forming the values by which she'd live her life. It was shortly after that that one of Claire's boyfriends had accused her of living a nun's existence, tauntingly called her "Mother Superior" when she'd rebuffed his advances by pointing out that Amy lay sleeping in the next room.

"Don't be angry," Amy entreated. "I didn't mean to get too nosy."

"Oh, baby, we don't have any secrets." The minute Claire spoke the words she knew they were no longer true. She averted her gaze as she fluffed her pillow. "Come on, let's go to sleep." She slid beneath the bedclothes, drew the sheets up to her chin, and closed her eyes tightly.

Why had she kissed him? When he lowered his head to adjust the stirrup, the dawning sun had glinted off the high ridge of his cheekbone and brushed it with a gentle shade of pink. Something had welled up inside her that she couldn't contain, and the kiss had been her release. Yet it had been such a hesitant kiss that she wondered if he'd felt it. Part of her sincerely hoped not.

The other part hoped he had.

"Davey Bohanon said the weather's going to break tomorrow," Amy offered. "He said this has been really cold for August around here and tomorrow it's going to heat up."

Claire rubbed her temples. "Who's Davey Bohanon? There's no one with the troupe by that name."

"He works for Jack," Amy told her, her tone warm

and dreamy. "Davey's *such* a fox. He tried to kiss me when we were hunting for Merlin."

"Uh-oh," Claire groaned, her eyes flying open.

"Relax. Nothing's going to happen."

"Oh, Amy, I—" Sometimes it was very hard being the guardian of a sixteen-year-old when she herself was only just twenty-six.

Amy found Claire's hand and squeezed it. "I love you, Cunky. I won't let you down. I'm so glad we're traveling the way you used to do with Mommy and Daddy. You're having fun, aren't you? Is it all you hoped it would be? I know you looked forward to it so much."

"Yes, Amy, it is," Claire murmured. "It's a wonderful life."

"I'm glad." Amy gave her another squeeze and rolled back over. "I love it too. Next month we go to Anaheim, right? I can't wait to see Disneyland!"

Claire swallowed. "Jack," she whispered.

"Did you say something?"

"Just good night."

"It's really morning." Amy snuggled against her pillow and yawned.

Soon she was snoring gently. But Claire, exhausted and drained as she was, couldn't fall asleep.

Claire tossed through the morning, the hammering of nails and scraping of saws filtering through fragmented dreams of night skies, moons, and horses. When she finally woke and sat up, it was stuffy in the trailer. The aroma of the dried flowers was thick and suffocating. Apparently Amy had awakened earlier, because the trailer was empty. Quickly Claire washed and dressed in a ruffled cotton skirt the color of cinnamon and a matching off-the-shoulder Gypsy blouse. Sliding her feet into leather sandals made by Old Tim the Cobbler, who usually erected his booth next to hers, she dabbed some scent behind her ears, brushed her hair, and secured it with a gauze bandanna.

Outside, she heard the clanking of bells and Lord Petit Sirrah's voice calling out the intricate patterns of a Morris dance for the six-member men's troupe that performed at the fair.

"Cross and cross!" he sang. "Forward three and back! Then swords up and—oh! good day, milord! I believe thy lady fair is yet abed. Shall I summon her?"

Claire opened the van door to find Jack mounted on Thunder, two perfectly matched white horses trailing behind.

"Ah, no need!" Petit Sirrah crooned. "Here be the lady now! 'Ah, that so light a foot could e'er outwear the everlasting flint!' "

Jack's smile as he looked at her was as bright as the sun that gleamed on his hatless head. His hair was a deep, rich brown frosted with streaks of blond, an uncanny match for his gold-flecked eyes. He looked vibrant and full of life, not at all like a man who had worked a full morning on a few hours sleep.

"God gi'good den," he hailed her, dismounting.

She smiled, not able to quell her happiness at seeing him, wondering again if he'd felt her kiss. "That means 'God give you a good evening,' " she said. She touched her hair to see if everything was in place. " 'Good morrow' will do."

"How about just plain 'howdy?' " Thunder danced toward her and Jack murmured, "How about 'I missed you so much I couldn't sleep?' "

Claire swallowed. Was that why she had lain awake though her body begged for rest? Because she yearned for Jack Youngblood?

He must have mistaken her silence for disapproval. A crooked smile dimpled one cheek as he said, "Guess I'd better stick to howdy."

One of the snow-white horses nickered in the ensuing pause. Claire gestured to them. "They're so lovely."

He held out the reins. "Arabians. They're for you

and Amy. I thought two Renaissance princesses should have their own mounts."

She blinked. "They're ours to use? All month?"

He nodded. "If you don't like them, I'll show you some others."

"Like them! I love them!" She raised shining eyes to him. "I can't believe it! Thank you, Jack!"

He was filled with pleasure at her delight. Leaning back in the saddle, he crossed his arms and watched as she allowed both horses to sniff her palms.

"That one's Pajaro and that one's Nieve. That means 'bird' and 'snow' in Spanish. Karen named them."

"Which one is easier to ride?"

His smile grew. "Amy will probably get on just fine with Pajaro. She's a good horse, not too speedy. Nieve's another proposition." Squint lines deepened around his eyes. "I thought you might enjoy a horse with some spirit."

"I've got to tell Amy," Claire said in a rush. "I'll just be a minute."

He held up his hand. "We'll tell her together. Mount up and we'll go find her."

Davey Bohanon had been right about the weather. The cool morning had been warmed by the sparkling sun. All around them the members of Claire's fair family were wearing cutoff jeans and T-shirts—all except Lord Petit Sirrah, who paraded in his velvet doublet and hose like a sweltering peacock. After a courtier's sweep of his porkpie hat he turned his attention back to his Morris dancers.

"Big doings," Jack observed. "The fair opens tomorrow, right?"

Claire didn't answer. He looked at her, to find her perched forward in the saddle, caressing the smooth, clean hide of Nieve. She was so engrossed, she looked as if she were in a trance, her slow, sensuous movements arousing to the man who watched her. She was communing with the mare, her breaths lengthy and deep, eyes half-closed. There was such depth to Claire van Teiler, he thought. It seemed he would never unpeel the many layers of the rose who sat beside him, and yet he felt somehow he knew her better than he knew any other person on earth.

She must have sensed his staring at her, for she quickly withdrew her hand. "I'm sorry, what did you say?"

"You open tomorrow."

"Uh-huh." She frowned as she looked at the English village rising on the green. "I don't know how we'll get it all done. Amy and I still have to put our booth up. Jack," she went on, pausing, "maybe we should visit your ranch another time."

"I'll send some help back with you later," he told her. "Just tell them what you want done and they'll take care of it."

"Claire!" Amy's high voice trilled. "Look at those horses!"

She ran toward them, dressed in white harem pants gathered at the ankles with lavender, purple, and pink ribbons, and a kimono blouse tied with an obi of the same colors. Circlets of dried flowers were looped around each wrist like massive bracelets, and she was carrying a pair of shears and a pincushion.

"Jack's lending them to us," Claire said. "This one's for you."

"My own horse?" She began to crouch down to inspect its underside.

"It's a mare," Jack drawled.

"Can I ride her?"

"That's what she's for." Jack dismounted easily and waved Amy over. "Here, let me help you up." When she pranced toward him, laughing, he shook his head and said, "Good grief, you're short."

Amy made a haughty face. "I'm taller than Claire."

He swung her into the saddle. "By what? A sixteenth of an inch?"

"Three whole inches. But she weighs more."

"You're right," Jack replied, winking at her. "About a sixteenth of a pound."

"By almost ten," Amy informed him.

Jack whistled. "What an old tub."

Amy cast a conspiratorial glance in Claire's direction. "Better watch out. You keep on like that and she'll let you have it."

Jack's eyes met Claire's. *That would be nice,* he wordlessly told her. Then he censored himself: *self-control, Youngblood.* This was the lady of his heart, not easily won. And perhaps not easily amused. He was sorry for that. He liked to tease, and to him a well-placed jibe gave him a sense of accomplishment.

But instead of looking insulted Claire was wrinkling her nose at the two of them and wagging her finger at Jack. "Watch it, cowboy," she snarled in a tone of mock menace. "Old tubs have been known to contain dynamite."

"I'd say you have an explosive personality," he rejoined.

"A short fuse," Amy agreed. "Be sure to keep matches away from her."

"Oh, I'm matchless." Jack grinned sassily at Claire. "Or so I've been told."

Claire tried to keep the red out of her cheeks but failed. "Come on. If we're going to get anything accomplished today, we'd better leave now."

"Where're we going?" Amy asked, bouncing her pincushion in her hand.

"We're *popping* over to my ranch," Jack said.

Amy clapped her hands. "Oh! I'm just *bursting* to see it!"

Jack tousled her hair in a brotherly way. "A fellow punster. How'd this kid get so smart?" he asked Claire.

Claire tapped herself on the chest. "Target practice. Now, *cannon* we get going? I'm not *gun* to stand here all day."

Jack and Amy groaned in unison. "Now I see where she gets it. Okay, let's take a *powder*. Come on, little sis." He gave Amy's horse a light smack, which sent Pajaro into a lope.

"She won't go very fast, will she?" Amy asked with concern. "I haven't ridden much."

"No, honey," Claire replied. "Jack picked her out specially for you."

"What a dynamite dude." Amy fluttered her lashes at him.

"No more puns!" Jack held up both hands and guided Thunder between the two ivory mares. "Truce. No more firing."

"Okay." Amy imitated the way Claire gathered up the reins, cradling the pincushion and scissors in her arms. "I'm all out of ammunition anyway."

"She's sharp," Jack said to Claire, who beamed proudly.

"Yes, she is."

"If you have some things to sew, why don't you bring them with you?" Jack suggested. "My sister can help and the work will go faster." And they would agree to stay longer, he thought.

"That's a great idea!" Amy said.

Claire shook her head. "You and your family have done enough for us already."

Jack regarded her. "Far from it, Lady Claire."

"I'll go get some stuff," Amy said. "Giddyup, Pajaro."

The horse whinnied and trotted away. Amy gave out a slightly panicked scream which turned into a cascade of giggles. Then she turned around and called, "I got you some tickets too!" Jack waved to show he'd heard.

"Really, I don't want to impose on your sister," Claire repeated.

"It won't be any trouble at all. Karen likes you. She wants to adopt Amy," he added, chuckling.

Claire sighed. "Everyone wants to adopt her. I wish she'd be a little more wary of strangers. She's too trusting."

"Seems to me you two run to extremes."

She raised her brows. "Meaning?"

He chewed the inside of his lip before responding. He fished in his pocket and pulled out a few jellybeans, offered them to her, and when she shook her head, fed them all to his horse.

"Meaning," he said finally, "that there *are* some strangers you can take candy from."

"Meaning?"

He saw the walls go up—the slight stiffening of the spine, the tightness around her mouth, the way her small hands gripped the reins. "Meaning I'm glad you're coming out to the ranch. How's your shoulder?"

"It's much better."

"Good."

She was still wary when Amy came back, laden with enough fabric and ribbons to keep a dozen people busy for a week. But in Amy's presence she relaxed again, and it occurred to Jack that part of Claire's protectiveness of her sister was really protectiveness of herself. She kept Amy close in order not to be alone. And Amy, bubbling and girlish, deflected the attention away from her elder sister and onto herself.

Oh, sweet Claire, he found himself thinking as he led the way toward his home, what has your life been like, to make you pull inside yourself like this?

The sisters rode side by side, Amy laughing and chattering, Claire answering in a pleasant but more subdued tone. Jack was the outsider, and he knew it. He rode a little ahead of them, trying not to eavesdrop, yet dying to know the cause of Claire's sudden fluttering of protest and Amy's high-pitched giggles.

Then both sisters spurred their horses to catch up with him, so they could ride three abreast on a trail beside the blacktop road. The air was loaded with the scent of apples, and an intriguing mixture of rose and lavender wafted from the circlets of flowers Amy had tied in a loop to her pommel.

"Are those hard to make?" he asked her, trying to make conversation.

Amy wrinkled her nose in superior fashion and untied one, handing it to him. "Not if you know how. We just wrap flowers around some wire and add some ribbons. The trick is knowing where to buy the flowers and how to twist them."

Jack examined it. "It looks like a halo." He pressed his thigh against Thunder's side, and the stallion side-stepped over to Nieve and sniffed at the mare. Thunder whinnied excitedly and tried to drop back, but Jack firmly held him in check. "We've got to watch these two," he said as he lowered the circlet onto the crown of Claire's shiny blond hair. The strands were baby-fine and delicate beneath his callused fingertips. "Thunder's not gelded."

"Is he a stud?" Amy piped up.

Jack chuckled. "Not officially."

"Then why don't you geld him?" she asked.

Jack touched the circlet, then trailed his fingers down her temple to touch the top of Claire's ear. He watched her lids flicker and felt a stirring deep in his loins. "I identify too closely with him maybe," he said, savoring the sensation that smoldered in his body, rising into his lower belly with steamy warmth. "Besides, I like a certain atmosphere at the ranch. The noncommercial stock can have babies whenever they want as far as I'm concerned. I think a little unbridled lust is a healthy thing. It communicates to the studs and the mares."

Amy squirmed in her saddle, giggling self-consciously, like a little child overhearing a dirty joke. Her behavior gave Jack pause. He'd forgotten how young she was.

But she wasn't *that* young. He noticed Claire giving her sister a silent command to settle down. Oh, who was he to criticize? he asked himself. He'd never had to raise a kid when he was just a kid himself.

Still, he couldn't help thinking that the lady of his heart was mother-henning her sister too much.

One day the little bird would leave the nest. He only hoped both sisters would be ready when that time came.

There was a brushing on his shoulder. He turned to find Claire leaning over toward him, straining to set the circlet on his head. Her cinnamon blouse was draped low on her shoulders, outlining her firm, high breasts, and her skirt fell in dainty ruffles around the saddle. He fell in love all over again.

"Hey, woman, what're you up to?" he said, laughing and gripping her wrist.

"Come on, let her do it!" Amy said. "You'd look so good. Just like a knight before a joust. Claire, let's make him a shirt and some bloomers."

"And some tights," Claire agreed, using her free hand to seize the circlet and toss it onto his head. Her eyes glittered and her high musical laugh filled the air. "There you go, milord cowboy. Now you're the King of the May."

"Treason!" Amy cried. "We already have a king!"

"The King of August then," Claire said. Her smile faded as Jack continued to hold her wrist. She caught her breath and swallowed, and it was all Jack could do to keep from taking her into his arms.

"How about the king of hearts?" he asked quietly.

They regarded each other. Energy surged between them, and Jack was enveloped by it, almost hypnotized. *If this were another century, I'd say she'd bewitched me,* he thought. *I'd say she made me fall in love with her. Because this isn't my style. It doesn't make sense.*

"The king of hearts?" he repeated in a whisper.

He let go of her wrist and she sank back into the saddle. As she did so he was certain that he saw her nod in agreement, that her huge cobalt eyes answered, *Yes, milord. You are my king of hearts.*

He gathered up the reins. If she doesn't stay, he thought, if she goes . . .

How could he lure this rare white dove to his nest? How could he make her love him?

His mind stopped whirling and his emotions took over until he was oblivious to everything but a hard, deep longing in his chest. When he looked up, the two sisters had trotted on ahead.

He reached out a hand. "My Claire," he said softly, "wait for me."

With a prod Thunder increased his pace. Just as Jack was about to catch up with them, Amy said, "Claire, look!"

"Oh!" Claire responded, and the two cantered over the crest of the hill.

"Hyah, Thunder!" The stallion broke into a full gallop, and Jack gave chase.

Four

"Jack, are these yours?" Claire called out as she and Amy cantered down the hill.

Behind a wooden fence, on a soft, verdant blanket of grass, dozens of miniature horses whinnied and frolicked. The tallest of the stallions was perhaps three feet high, and the foals looked like stuffed toys for a child's nursery. Most of them were a rosy antelope-beige, their shaggy manes of cream or white flying behind them as they capered and pranced.

"Mini-neighs!" Amy squealed. "Claire, help me get off my horse. I want to play with them."

"I'm not sure if you should."

"It's fine." Jack rode up beside Amy and took the reins from her. "These belong to my next-door neighbor. Jess won't mind if you take a closer look at them."

"They're so tiny," Claire said, dismounting. "I've never seen anything like them."

Sliding off Thunder, Jack joined them, gallantly opening the gate and allowing the sisters to enter before him. As Claire passed she looked up at him. He towered in the center of the sky. The gilt orb of the sun gleamed directly behind his head, the beams diffusing around him and softening his rough-hewn, earthy features. His tanned skin fairly glowed with the beauty of the day, with aliveness and a kinship with his surroundings. A sharp yearning swelled within her and she quickly looked away, focusing her attention on catching up with Amy.

"Help! Help!" Amy whooped as a ring of curious horses surrounded her, tugging at the ribbons on her blouse and harem pants. At the sound of her clear soprano voice they scampered away, only to be replaced by another ring of the mythical-looking creatures.

"Back, you little chickens!" Claire ordered, shooing them like pesky birds. The bantam steeds wheeled away, then, undaunted, returned to inspect the new arrivals once more. They worried Claire's long skirt, their tails whisking against her calves. She caught one around its neck and wagged her finger in its face. Two doelike eyes gazed mischievously back at her.

"Stop this commotion," she told it, bending down to meet it eye to eye. It took a step forward, forcing her to rock back on her heels. "Just stand still and let me get to know you."

In answer it licked her cheek like a puppy. Claire made a face, and behind her Jack chuckled deep in his throat.

"Here, let me help," he offered.

Crouching behind her, he balanced himself by resting one hand on her shoulder, and with the other reached around her to the audacious little creature. Claire smelled leather and musk and a special odor all Jack's own, an essence of maleness that enticed her senses. His long, strong fingers stroked the muzzle of the horse, then scratched between its ears as one would pet an affectionate Irish setter.

The animal began to quiet. "Easy, easy," Jack murmured, and a heavy fringe of lashes around the horse's liquid eyes blinked once, twice, three times at the gentle, low voice. "Here, little one." He dug into his pocket and produced a jellybean. "Jess won't mind a couple," he said, excusing himself for feeding the horse candy.

The little thing sniffed the sweet, then gobbled it up. It whinnied in a falsetto imitation of a normal-size horse and searched Jack's palm for more.

"Here, honey, you feed him this time," Jack said, and gave a jellybean to Claire.

The muzzle was like velvet. The horse snatched up the candy and took a step forward, butting Claire's shoulder in a demand for more.

"Ow!" Claire cried involuntarily, flinching from the pain. She began to fall backward, but Jack's steadying hand caught her against his chest. His legs spread to accommodate her and she was wedged between hard, muscular thighs encased in faded blue jeans.

"Are you all right?" he demanded, concern making his voice husky and deep. He touched her shoulder. When she hunched forward he cupped his hand and massaged the sore spot in a gentle, circular motion. At once the constricted sinews and nerves relaxed.

"Thanks." She tried to move out of his embrace, but he wouldn't let her go. A fluid warmth, like fine brandy, began to spread from her shoulder down her arm and across her chest. Her collarbones, her neck, her breasts all awakened, as if touched by his expert caress. Her nipples contracted to two ripe buds that belied the softness of her feminine form, and she was aware that as Jack fondled and stroked her shoulder his fingers were a hairbreadth away from them. Her eyes closed, and she felt her body whispering, *Touch them. Touch all of me.*

His heart thundered against her shoulder blades and his breathing became shallow. The muscles in his thighs tightened and his body arched forward slightly, as if with a primitive yearning to bury himself inside her responsive flesh—

"You guys!" Amy cried. "Look what I found!"

Claire snapped out of her trance. My Lord, she

thought, what were they doing? They'd practically been making love right in the middle of the pasture!

Jack swore under his breath. His chest heaving, he stood and carefully raised her to a standing position, as mindful of her as he had been of his baby niece.

"Come here!" Amy called again. She was standing in a copse of pine trees with one chain of daisies on her head and another around the neck of a small goat.

"We'll continue this later," Jack murmured, taking Claire's hand and raising it to his lips. The gold in his eyes flashed as he kissed her knuckles with dry, smooth lips. His strong will cast its shadow over Claire, overwhelming her power to refuse. His desire was thick in the air, but within it warm-hearted caring burned strong and true.

Claire sucked in her breath and raised her chin. "What did you find, sweetie?" she called to Amy.

"A wife for Merlin!" Amy shouted back. "Look how friendly she is!"

Claire moved away from Jack. "She's just the right size too!" she said, laughing as the goat butted Amy and she stumbled forward. Without looking at Jack, Claire hurried toward the pair.

"We'll continue," Jack said loudly enough for her to hear, but she pretended not to as she ran from the imposing man to the sanctuary of her sister's company.

Then, almost as if he'd spoken aloud, she heard Jack saying, *Just remember, my lady Claire, you can't run forever.*

After admiring the goat the three of them mounted their horses and cut across the paddock of Jessie Reynolds's miniature-horse farm toward Rancho Espejo, Jack's home. Amy's caution toward her horse had completely evaporated, and she merrily led the way, echoing the songs of the birds in the treetops. Claire and Jack rode behind her in silence, each lost in thought. The rhythm of the horses' hooves was a counterpoint to their heartbeats. Claire wondered if she would ever draw a deep breath again. Her chest was so tight and sensitive, she couldn't seem to inhale deeply.

But when Rancho Espejo appeared beyond the trees she forgot herself and cried out.

"Oh, it's beautiful!"

Two large practice rings preceded lengths of freshly painted enclosed stables. Other wooden buildings abutted them, and beyond everything else loomed a huge Spanish-style mansion three stories tall, crowned with a tile roof of rich terra cotta. Arched windows dressed in stained glass gleamed above a massive carved oak door that promised more luxury within. Sturdy pepper trees and graceful oaks shaded an emerald lawn and brick patio set with scores of pots of plump, gaudy geraniums and pansies.

As Claire gaped, a stablehand emerged from one of the more distant buildings leading a magnificent chestnut mare. Beside him, a model-thin woman dressed in jodhpurs, English riding boots, and a dark cap laid a proprietary hand on the horse's neck.

"Oh, good, the baroness has arrived," Jack said. He turned to Claire with an expectant expression. "Well, what do you think?"

She gestured with her hands. "I had no idea you were so rich."

He shrugged. "A few good investments."

A few good investments. And she had thought him some itinerant handyman back at the antique shop.

"It's stunning," she said sincerely. "You must be very proud."

"I guess I am." He cocked his head as he surveyed his domain. "It's taken a lot of years, but ranching's all I know." A breeze ruffled his hair, shooting gold through it like silken thread. "That and income tax forms," he added, laughing. "I have the fastest calculator in the West. Now maybe you don't feel so bad about letting me pay your doctor's bill."

She shook her head. "I'm proud too."

"I know," he said softly. "I admire you for that."

"Well, you're certainly settled in here," she went on, her voice getting high as she grew nervous. The exquisite house seemed to pull her like a magnet. "You won't be going anyplace soon, while everything Amy and I own is stuffed in that van and—"

"And are you satisfied with that?"

She gave a toss of her head. "There's more to life than material possessions."

"Oh, I quite agree." His eyes glittered. "I'm glad you like my home."

"It seems more like a palace."

"Fit for a princess. There's even a music room," he added, curbing Thunder's head with a practiced tug. The stallion was intent on trotting for the stable, where there would be fresh hay and water and freedom from the weight of the saddle. "And a greenhouse, where Karen grows orchids."

"Does she live with you?"

He shook his head. "No, she and her husband have an apartment over the antique shop. In fact, you slumbered in their bed, Goldilocks. Remember?"

The four-poster with the sunny quilt. The smells of lemon, wax, and violets. And the stallion eyes of a compelling stranger . . .

"Yes, yes, I do," she said softly.

Cantering ahead, Amy greeted the exquisite baroness, and the woman stopped. They began talking animatedly, though they were too far away for Claire to hear their voices. Then Amy slid off her horse and gestured to the woman's head. The baroness took off her riding cap and popped it on Amy's head, laughing.

"Karen and her husband are coming over tonight for dinner," Jack added. "You can meet him then."

"Oh, we can't possibly stay that long," Claire

said. "We have so much to do before tomorrow!" She knit her brows. "I hope Amy isn't making a nuisance of herself."

"I'm sure she isn't," Jack replied easily. He touched Claire's hair. "Hey, loosen the reins a little," he murmured. "You're held in too tightly. Life doesn't have to be a struggle."

Claire could feel the movements of his fingers as he played with the lock of her hair. Her scalp tingled and her face grew warm. To counteract his effect on her, she busied herself with the reins.

"You don't know anything about my life."

"I know enough to know I can make you smile again."

"What do you mean? I smile all the time."

"Not in your heart, Cunky." Jack combed his fingers through her hair, the tips grazing the nape of her neck. "Your eyes look sad, even when you're laughing." He slowly encircled the back of her neck and rubbed it. "Let me in, Lady Claire."

Holding the reins in her hand, she flashed him an overbright smile and swung her leg over the saddle, forcing him to move away. "Sorry, there's no room in the inn," she said lightly. "Now, do we get the nickel or the dime tour?"

"Claire, don't close me out."

She touched her hair and discovered her bandanna was loose. As she reached up to retie the ends Jack caught her hands and lowered them to her lap. As he gazed at her he untied the scarf and drew it slowly away from her hair.

"You've got to let me in," he said.

You're already in, she wanted to reply, but she said nothing, only took the bandanna from him and folded it between her hands.

Jack sighed. "You're not making this very easy."

She touched his arm. Her eyes were two huge pools, clear and blue and deep. "Then give up, Jack. Please. For both our sakes. Nothing can come of . . . anything between us. In a month I'll be gone. I couldn't stand . . ." She trailed off. She'd already said too much. She knew that if he realized she was half in love with him already, he would persist in his attentions. Each touch, each look from him was like a battering ram pounding on her heart. But she couldn't give in to his siege, not when the inevitable result of her capitulation would be heartbreak.

She had promised to show Amy the wide world, and this was the time in her young life when she needed Claire most. This was her year of freedom, and Claire would not desert her.

She looked at her sister, who had handed back the cap to the baroness, then nodded vigorously and waved as the woman strode on willowy legs to catch up with her horse. When she saw Claire she waved and began to hurry toward her and Jack.

"I'll have someone show you the house," Jack said gruffly, interrupting her reverie. "I need to speak with the baroness for a while. She'll want to leave before dark."

Claire felt cut by his impersonal tone. Well, it was what she'd wanted, she reminded herself, wasn't it? "We need to leave soon too," she added.

His eyes flashed. She saw real anger in them. He dismounted, then held his arms out for her. She was sitting on the saddle with her legs dangling over the left side of Nieve. Reluctantly, yet with a thrill of sensual pleasure, she slid down the horse's flank and allowed Jack to circle her waist.

His grip was like iron. His eyes were hot enough to melt steel. He held her for the briefest of moments. A muscle jumped in his cheek and, for a sharp heartbeat, Claire thought—or hoped—he was going to kiss her.

Instead, he lowered her to the earth. "Claire," he said heavily, then turned from her and gathered up the reins of both horses. He handed them to a stablehand and gently pressed the small of Claire's back, guiding her toward the house. "Ask Davey to come up here," he said over his shoulder to the cowboy.

"Hi, guys," Amy said, rushing up to them. "Gosh, Jack, that woman is a baroness!"

"Yes, I know," Jack replied wryly.

"And you live in a *mansion*! Wouldn't you like to live here, Cunky? Is there a Jacuzzi?"

Jack laughed. "Yes, there is."

"Oh, we'll have to bring our bathing suits next time! I *love* Jacuzzis," Amy said enthusiastically.

"I'm sure we have an extra suit around here that would fit you," Jack said. He glanced at Claire, then went on. "In fact, after dinner we could all go in if you'd like."

"Are we staying for dinner?" Amy asked, looking at Claire.

Claire glanced at Jack and then exhaled slowly. He was baiting the hook with her sister. "I think not," she said stiffly.

"Oh, please!"

Claire folded her arms. "Amy, we have to get ready for the opening."

"But Jack will help us, won't you?" At his nod she smiled triumphantly. "He must have twenty guys around here. All we need is one to help put the sides of the booth up." She laughed. "I mean, heck, if Lord Petit Sirrah can manage it, one of these big guys should have no problem."

"My thinking exactly," Jack said.

Claire set her jaw. "Oh, come on," Amy urged. "We've been eating canned stuff for weeks."

"We're having steak and ribs," Jack put in.

"*Steak!*" Amy clutched her hands together in an attitude of supplication. "Claire, *steak*!"

And ribs, Claire's favorite. He was beguiling her, she thought, studying the animated face of her sister. Just like the serpent, in this town that was a garden of ripening apples.

"All right," she said ungraciously. "You win."

"Hurray!" Amy cried.

Jack smiled at Claire and plopped Amy's daisy crown over her brown eyes. "Good for you, little sis," he said. "You succeeded where others failed."

Giggling, Amy took off the circlet and pulled one of the daisies from it. "You just have to know how to handle her," she advised Jack. She tore off two creamy petals in succession.

"Loves me, loves me not," Jack recited, watching her.

She nodded, mouthing the words as she tore off more. The trio walked on.

As they were approaching the patio a short young man with flaming red hair and leather chaps over his jeans emerged from the side of the house and waved at Amy.

"Oh!" Amy's clear voice rang through the yard. "Hi, Davey!"

"Hey, your majesty," Davey answered, doffing his cowboy hat.

"Well, well, well," Jack drawled. "I didn't know we had a little romance going on here." He took the flower from Amy's grasp. There were three petals left. "I thought you were thinking of *me* while you were doing this."

Amy gave him a saucy look. "Yeah, I'll bet."

"Where were you up to?" he asked, twirling the stem.

"Loves me. Hey, Davey, neat chaps." She left Jack's side to meet the redheaded cowboy halfway.

Jack plucked the next petal. "Loves me not." The second. "Loves me." The third. "Loves me not." He let the flower fall to the dirt.

"Yeah, I'll bet," he said, and smiled wickedly at Claire.

Jack left Claire and Amy in the custody of Davey, who was alternately nervous, flirtatious, and proud as he showed off his boss's house. He led them through the airy spaces, down whitewashed corridors, and through spacious rooms decorated in Mexican-Colonial style, up the three flights of tiled steps to the library, more guest rooms, and Jack's private quarters.

"This is his office," he informed them, pushing open a carved door. "It links with his bedroom."

"Oh, wow," Amy murmured as they entered the office.

A huge oak desk, its surface bare except for a computer and a calculator, sat diagonally facing the doorway. Behind it, exquisite oils of equally exquisite horses covered the walls. Enclosed in glass cases were blue ribbons and signed letters from celebrities and other prominent people, thanking Jack for the services of his farm. A profusion of plants dangled from the ceiling, casting lacy shadows on the woven Indian rugs spread on the shining hardwood floor.

"Let's see his bedroom," Amy said, and Davey obligingly opened another door.

As Claire passed through she caught her sleeve on the curved brass arm of an oak hatrack. As she freed herself she noted the many cowboy hats settled there, and crowning them—like a Christmas tree star—was the circlet of wildflowers she'd been wearing during the chase after Merlin.

He kept it, she thought wonderingly, pleased and flustered.

Then she stepped into his bedroom, and this time it was her turn to murmur her appreciation.

A huge brass bed gleamed beneath a skylight made of stained glass. There was brass and copper everywhere, and marble-topped chests and a freestanding mirror framed by carved oak birds and trees. Painted porcelain chandeliers made her think of muted twilights, languid sensuous evenings.

"Fancy meeting you here," Jack said softly behind her. When she spun around to face him she realized they were alone. Davey and Amy had vanished.

"Where's my sister? They were just here."

He smiled. "She's fine. There's lots more to see." Still smiling, he shut the door.

"You sent them away!"

With a twist of his hand he locked the door. "So much more to see." He cupped her chin in the curl of his fingers, stroking the flesh beneath her jaw. She could feel the calluses on his fingertips as he trailed his fingers down her neck. "I want to show you my world, Claire. I want you to see that life is for finding happiness, for . . . love."

"Let me go." Her lips moved, but no sound came from them. She tried to clear her throat, but she couldn't. It was as if he'd hypnotized her, holding her spellbound as he caressed her neck and shoulders. The gold flecks in his eyes danced like dust motes in the sunlight. Above them the skylight misted soft pinks and lavenders on his face. He was so masculinely beautiful and his touch was so enthralling that she couldn't fight him anymore.

Couldn't fight herself. Never, in all the lonely days, the celibate nights, had she been consumed so completely by her own passion. She had no weapons with which to resist the force of her desire—and his.

Still, she fought. Summoning all her strength of will, she tried to raise a hand to push him away. But her body was no longer her own. It was like lead, and she was a burning, throbbing statue coming to life under his ardor. Her head fell back against his waiting hand while his other hand wrapped under her ear and across her neck.

She caught her breath as his lips pressed against hers. Soft and warm, pliant and careful, his mouth roamed over hers, exploring it, claiming it. His shaking fingers traced the hollows of her cheeks, the bridge of her nose, her earlobe. The sheer pleasure of his touch parted her lips, and a sharp thrill of lightning shot up her spine when he slid his tongue into her mouth.

He tasted like sugar, she thought dreamily. With scarcely controlled passion he was probing her inner recesses, seeking out the tender, sensitive places that made her shiver in his arms.

The first kiss ended, followed by another and another. Gasping, Claire was vaguely aware that she was clinging to him and that they were sinking, as if in slow motion, onto the big brass bed.

He was easing her down. The thick mattress compressed beneath their combined weight, and they were nearly submerged in the fleecy smoothness. Claire was floating and blazing. Her back was tightly arched, and as her head touched the tan and blue bedspread, his chest pressed against her breasts. The taut points of her nipples were so sensitive, it seemed as though she were naked. She felt the wrinkles and buttons on his shirt as he undulated against her.

His weight forced her back into the mattress and as she lay beneath him, he urged her legs apart and rocked against the thin fabric of her skirt. She wasn't wearing a slip, only a pair of fawn-colored bikinis, and the heat of his desire permeated her feminine being. A match struck against flint—a fire flared inside—and she gave a little cry.

"Jack, oh, Jack," she moaned. "Please stop. I don't want to do this."

Despite his passion he chuckled. "Yeah, I'll bet."

"Please, my sister—"

He replied by cupping a hand over her breast. Claire leaped beneath him, her fingers digging into his back.

"Such fire beneath the icy surface," he murmured, fitting his palm over the quickening bud. "You want me as much as I want you. I think it's been this way since the moment we first laid eyes on each other." With slow, irresistible movements he fondled the fleshy roundness, encircling it with his fingers, lifting and kneading it. "I don't know how you hold your passion in like you do, but I can't wait to unleash it."

"Jack . . ."

He moved to her other breast, then flattened his hand over her stomach. With a slight pressure he pushed down on it, and an intense, erotic thrill centered there and fanned outward through her entire body. Flames danced inside her, heating her blood, searing away the layers of fear and inhibition. She wanted him. Hungrily, fiercely, she had to have him.

They were both panting. A soft sheen of perspiration covered Claire's brow, and she was hot beyond belief, sweltering in her clothing. *Soon*, her mind begged. *Cool me, soon.*

But there was no release from the heat and the wanting. He continued to kiss and fondle her, and his hand gathered her skirt gently up her legs, searching for the treasure of her womanhood.

"My flower," he whispered. "My lady orchid."

Her chest heaved with her shallow breathing. When his knowing hand caressed her intimately she thought she would faint from the joy of it. She was open and ready. She had blossomed for him. At that moment she was his lady, his love, whatever he wanted her to be.

Jack raised his head and looked at her. He was breathing rapidly. His nostrils flared with the effort, and he reminded her again of a great stallion preparing himself to take her.

She saw him gather his thoughts together, and then, in a slow, measured tone, he asked, "Are you on the pill?"

She grimaced. In the white heat of passion she had forgotten that she was unprotected. Yet she was glad he had cared enough to remember.

"Claire?"

Averting his face, she shook her head.

He took three breaths, exhaling deeply each time. "It's all right," he said. "I'll take care of it."

He pulled open a nightstand drawer and began to rummage through it. She saw a flash of pink lace—some other woman's panties? she thought—and a glimmer of silver foil.

"No," she said quickly, sitting up. "No, this is going too far. I can't believe I was doing this!"

He kissed her lips. "Believe in us," he said. "Claire, keep believing. Don't worry. Amy's off somewhere with Davey."

Claire frowned. "Stop using her like that. Don't try to get to me through her. If she gets a crush on that cowboy, it'll break her heart when we have to leave."

He was silent for a moment, obviously struggling with himself. Then he reached down and pulled up her blouse, deftly unfastening her lacy bra before she knew what he was doing.

Lowering his head to her breast, he licked the rosy center and the blushing point. His hair was like velvet against her skin as he suckled like a child, holding her shoulders when she struggled beneath him.

"If we made a baby, would you stay?" he asked. His eyes were stormy.

Shocked, she stared at him.

"Because maybe I just should . . ." Her skirt was bunched around her hips and he searched impatiently through the folds of gauze for the waistband of her panties. When he found it he looped his fingers around it as if he were going to tear the bikinis off.

"Jack," she said, gasping, astonished by his ferocity.

Her voice checked him. Immediately he let go of her clothes and ran a hand through his hair.

"Damn." He touched her cheek. "I don't want to have self-control, Claire, especially where you're concerned." He grinned crookedly. "I guess I got used to sex stud-farm style. If I wanted it, I got it. All the other . . ." He waved a hand, unwilling to finish the thought.

The mood was shattered, the walls back up around her heart. She swung her legs over the opposite side of the bed, straightened her clothes, and walked on unsteady legs toward the door.

Jack jumped up. "Claire, wait. I think you misunderstood what I was saying. What I meant was—"

"I don't care what you meant," she said, hurrying through the office. *You're running again,* she accused herself. *Will you spend your whole life running?*

Yes, if need be, she heard the silent answer.

" 'My true love roams the wide world 'round.
'round and 'round and through the glen.
My true love wears a shield of gold;
My love is king among all men.

My true love roams the wide world 'round.
'round and 'round and o'er the sea,
Oh, blow ye winds into his sails.
And blow my true love back to me.' "

"Oh, that's beautiful," Karen said, clapping as Claire's and Amy's voices died away and the guitar chord thrummed into silence. "And that's from the seventeenth century, you say?"

"Uh-huh," Amy told her. "We learned it in Rhode Island."

"You've been everywhere," Tom, Karen's husband, put in.

"Just about," Amy agreed. She lifted her head from Claire's shoulder. "But we still have all kinds of places to go, right Cunky?"

They were sitting in Jack's living room before a small fire in the massive brick fireplace. The night air was cool enough to make it enjoyable, though Jack had opened some windows to keep the room from becoming too warm.

Karen and Tom lounged on horsehair couches, sipping apple wine. Claire perched on a large stuffed pillow, her skirts spread around her, Amy beside her on another pillow with a pile of finished sachets in her lap. Jack sat in a rocker nearer the fire. He was smiling down at Megan, who was snuggled in his arms.

"That did the trick," he said with satisfaction.

"It's not every night she gets a lullaby in two-part harmony," Karen said.

"More like every night, *we* get the " 'wah-wah-wah-wah chorus,' " Tom added ruefully.

"Now, guys, stop picking on my niece." Jack set down a baby bottle, a rattle, and a stuffed poodle, and began to rise. "I'll put her down in the other room. Claire, would you like to help?"

Speculative eyes were on her as she nodded and stood. Jack put his free arm around her, cradling Megan in the crook of the other one, and they walked together out of the room.

"Now, that's a pretty sight," she overheard Karen say. "Like a little family. Jack's so good with kids."

"So's my sister," Amy piped up.

"Gossips," Jack drawled to Claire. He opened a door and gestured for Claire to precede him.

"There's a night-light on the dresser," he whispered.

She turned it on, enchanted to find herself in a nursery. Pastel horses galloped over rainbows as moons and suns beamed down on them. Clowns and balloons announced that this was "Megan's Room" in huge letters across the ceiling.

But the thing that touched her most was the old wooden cradle, newly painted white with "Megan" spelled at the foot. She imagined a farmer from years ago carving it by the firelight, smiling at his pregnant wife. Wistfully she traced the smooth curve of the headboard and pushed on the side, making it rock.

"Oh, shoot," Jack murmured. "I forgot to change the sheets." He sighed. "Claire, would you mind holding her while I get some clean ones?"

"I'd love to."

She held her arms out for the sleeping child, and the moment Megan's satiny face pressed against Claire's breast, something happened inside her. A deep, abiding peace filled her heart, and she was filled with love for the sweet, trusting soul that rested in her embrace. As she touched Megan's tiny, perfect fingers, marveling at the nails, Jack's words came rumbling through her mind: *If we made a baby . . .*

He had left the room in search of the sheets, so she felt free to let two tears of emotion course down her cheeks. A baby. A sharp longing rose in her to have one. To have Jack's.

And then she overheard Amy from the next room, regaling Tom and Karen with stories of their adventures.

"Next we're going to Anaheim, and then we're going to San Francisco! It's so great! Claire used to live like this all the time, and we waited and waited until I was old enough. And we're having so much fun!"

"But don't you ever wish you had a real home?" Karen asked.

"Graduating at sixteen. A smart girl like you should be in college," Tom added.

"Oh, I'll go someday. But we just got started. You can't imagine how long we've been dreaming about doing this. Hey, Karen, is that smocking? Will you teach me how to do that?"

"Sure, Amy. You'll pick it up in no time. You're a clever seamstress."

"Thanks. I love sewing. I love it when we get costume orders. It's my favorite thing."

Two more tears trickled down Claire's cheeks. She was weaving silly fantasies. She knew her place and what she must do. Smiling sadly, she kissed Megan's downy head and held her close.

Jack bustled back in. "Mission accomplished!" he said softly, holding up a fresh set of bed linen.

Busily he set to work, pulling the soiled sheets off and wrapping the little mattress in new ones. Claire watched his back and arm muscles shifting in the pale light, heard his breathy, tuneless whistling, evidence of his pleasure in the task.

If we made a baby . . .

"We need to go back to the fairgrounds soon," she whispered. "It's getting late."

He paused and looked up at her. She could read his thoughts—he had hoped they would make love later in the evening, despite her protests that afternoon. He opened his mouth to say something, then pressed his lips tightly together and finished making the bed.

Megan stirred when Claire laid her down on her back. The baby clamped a hand around Claire's little finger and began to suck on it. Gently Claire extricated herself and tenderly drew a fuzzy pink blanket beneath Megan's chin. She began to straighten up, then bent back down to brush wispy curls from Megan's smooth forehead.

"Good night, honey," she murmured, giving Megan's hand a squeeze.

When she raised her head she saw Jack standing in the doorway watching her.

"If it would do any good, I'd lock you in here with her," he said.

Do it, Claire wanted to tell him. But then she realized what that would mean.

Not only would she have no way out, but Amy would have no way in.

Five

Surreptitiously Claire rubbed the ice cube between her breasts and let the ice water trickle down. "Sweet lavender and thyme!" she called. "Favors for a lady's chamber! Satins and rosebuds!"

Excitement coursed through her veins. The fair had been open for less than an hour and the grounds were packed with visitors. They were scouring the mock village, inspecting everything contained within the perimeter of the high wooden wall. Above their heads flapped the bright green and white pennants emblazoned with the crest of Their Majesties of the May—three ravens, three dragons *passant guardant*, and their motto, translated as "We Revel!" The food and crafts booths bulged with people, looking—and buying, thank goodness, Claire noted—and an expectant throng had formed around the Festival Stage, awaiting the arrival of Their Majesties and their royal court.

It was blistering hot. Davey Bohanon had forgotten to mention the imminent arrival of a California Santa Ana. Scorching air from the north had burned away the balminess of the day before, leaving weather so sweltering the earth shimmered. The only remedies available to Claire and Amy were well-placed ice cubes, soaked washclothes, and hats.

"Thank goodness we decided to 'wench it,' " Claire said to Amy during a brief lull in business. Both were wearing the clothes of country maidens: Claire's gauze skirts of blue, white, and brown were hiked almost to her knees beneath a cinnamon apron. One of her billowy blouses clung to her moist skin, and her ice cube was kept solidly in place by the tight lacings of her leather waistcoat. She and Amy wore huge cartwheel hats of straw decorated with flowers and draped with huge white squares of cloth to protect the backs of their necks and shoulders. Though they would have preferred to go barefoot, leather sandals were tied around their ankles with thongs.

"I, too, am glad we have clothed ourselves like peasants," Amy replied, using the formal, old-fashioned English required by Lord Petit Sirrah when they were in costume. She was dressed much like Claire, though in shades of green, like a Renaissance Tinker Bell, Claire thought fondly. "Lavender and thyme!" she called, holding two sachets in her hands. "Oh, Mistress Claire, I fain would faint from this heat."

Perching on the edge of a trestle table laden with their wares, Claire cooled first herself, then Amy, with a huge wooden fan shaped like a paddle. "I would fain as well. But thou knowest what they say."

"What say they?"

Claire grinned. " 'No fain, no gain.' "

They giggled. "I pray the horses of milord Jack do bear this heat with a good will," Amy said.

"I pray so also. Didst feed them this morn?" Jack had brought over plenty of hay and water, and his cowboys had built a small but sturdy corral for Nieve and Pajaro. Lord Petit Sirrah was very pleased with the addition to the village, and agreed to assign watches over them while Amy and Claire worked their booth.

"Aye, sister, I did."

A woman indicated she wanted to purchase a pillow, one of the many they'd stayed up so late to finish. Claire clipped off the price tag while Amy took the woman's money and counted out the change. As the woman left with her treasure, they curtsied, saying, "Thank'ee, milady."

"We have made enough already this day to keep us for half a fortnight in canned chili," Amy said, riffling through their wicker cash box.

" 'Tis a wondrous thing, mistress," Claire replied happily. "Our good fortune is made by thy good needle."

"And also by thy good voice, for later we must needs sing for the court and pass the hat," Amy reminded her. She sidled up to Claire and squeezed her hand. "I'm having such a good time, Cunky," she whispered. "Thank you for doing all this for me."

Claire squeezed back. "For us," she corrected her sister. "I'm having just as much fun as you are. Maybe more."

"That's impossible."

"Hey, how much for this flower thing?" a man called out, and Claire hurried away to help him.

"Why, sir, that be a mere five crowns," she said.

"Five bucks! For *this*?"

"What a great deal!" said a familiar masculine voice behind Claire. She shivered at the low, delicious tones and the husky rasp. "They were eight down at that other booth."

The man looked past Claire to Jack. "Really?"

"Yeah. My sister almost bought a dozen for her antique shop. I'm glad she waited. I'll send her down here."

Jack looked spectacular that morning, Claire thought, though not at all like a rancher. A blue and white rugby shirt molded his chest, tight white denims cradled his hips, and the appealing combination ended in white sneakers on his sockless feet. The stark white contrasted with his tanned skin, the softness of the shirt with the straight lines of his hips and legs. As she looked at him Claire felt the last of her ice cube dribble away, leaving her flushed and warm.

"Well, then I guess I'll take one too," the man said, obviously pleased he'd gotten a bargain.

"They're going fast," Jack warned him. "They had twice this many when they opened."

"Two, then," the man said.

Claire curtsied. "Thank'ee sir," she murmured, glancing at Jack. "Doth that be check or cash?"

"Do you take credit cards?"

"Alack, no."

"Doesn't matter. Here's a ten."

She inclined her head. "My humble gratitude."

The man chuckled. "This whole thing is weird, but it's interesting. Beats mowing the lawn anyhow."

He walked away. Claire turned to Jack and waved a finger at him. "Sir, thou art a wondrous fibber. There be no other booth selling garlands."

He shrugged his shoulders. "So I exaggerated."

"Thou art a shill, sir."

"I art a businessman. You two look like candy-box shepherdesses."

Amy batted her eyelashes outrageously at him. "And thou lookest like Magnum, P. I."

"Really, Lady Amy?" Jack posed, thrusting out his chest and hooking a thumb through a low-slung belt loop.

Amy giggled. "For shame, sir. Today we be wenches, not ladies!"

"Oh? So what do I call you?"

"We are Mistress Amy and Mistress Claire, at thy service."

"Hey, how much are these flower things?" asked a girl with purple hair and a cross tattooed on her forehead.

"Hoo boy," Amy murmured, turning her attention to the girl. Jack grinned wickedly at Claire and said, "So today you're my *Mistress* Claire?"

Claire began to rearrange the pillows and sachets on the table. "No more than I'm at your service."

"That's a tricky word in my line of work," he drawled. When she frowned, puzzled, he said, "Servicing. Speaking of which, we bred the baroness's mare this morning."

"Congratulations."

"Wild stuff. Amy would have gone into hysterics."

Claire tried to suppress her smile and failed. "Amy's very curious about nature."

"I'm a nature boy myself." He leaned his forearm on a rack of exquisite costumes made of rich velvets and brocades, a position which afforded him, Claire knew, a splendid view of her cleavage.

"You are too bold, sir." She moved away, straightening a box of sachets.

He chewed the inside of his cheek. "Sometimes I wonder if I'm bold enough."

"Stop wondering."

"So, what'll we have for dinner tonight?"

Claire moved the box to another part of the table. "Amy and I should eat here. It's the first night after the fair and Lord P. S. will want to see how everybody did."

As if on cue, the midget walked up, shaking his finger at her. "For shame, mistress! All members of our band must needs speak proper English!"

She inclined her head. "Forgive me, milord. I had forgot."

"See that in future thou—" He looked up, noticing Jack for the first time, and he smiled brightly. "Ah, good day, milord. Art disporting thyself?"

Jack considered. "Yes, I think so."

Lord P. S. bowed. "Pray, do not allow one such as I to interrupt." With a flourish he drew his velvet cape over his arm and strutted away.

Jack grinned. "I think that guy's on my side."

"I fain would hope. Else I shall be fined ten crowns for speaking with an unseemly tongue," Claire said.

"Ten bucks?"

"Aye, milord. We of the fair must speak as in the olden days."

"Is that a condition of employment? Where'd you learn it, Berlitz?"

She chuckled. "Nay, milord. Lord P. S. hath taught us all."

"Lord P. S. is really into this."

"Aye, sir."

"Well, if you won't come for dinner, will you come for dessert?"

"I think not, sir. We must needs rest."

"We'll have angel food cake. Light stuff, requires little effort to lift yon fork to yon mouth."

She sighed. "Oh, Jack. Please, I can't . . ." She pulled a damp washcloth from her bodice and dabbed at her forehead. "I have to—"

She stopped speaking as Jack whipped his head to the left, a startled expression speading over his features. He ran to the other end of the table and grabbed Amy by the shoulders.

"Are you all right?" he demanded of her, shoving the tattooed girl out of the way. A garland dropped from the purple hair to the ground.

Claire rushed to Amy's side. Her little sister was chalk-white.

"It must be the heat," Claire said. "Honey, sit down."

"No, Cunky," Amy breathed. "I'm all right." Laughing unsteadily, she rubbed her temples. "I'm sorry. I was being dumb."

"Sit down," Jack ordered.

Amy laid a hand on his arm. "It's okay, Jack. I just thought I saw somebody I know."

A look passed between her and Claire. Claire could feel Jack intercept it and try to decipher it.

"Aunt Norma?" she murmured. Amy nodded.

"But it wasn't," Amy assured her. "Just somebody who looked like her. Oops, here comes Lord P. S. again. We must needs speak in the proper way."

She bustled back to the purple-headed girl.

Claire stood before Jack with folded hands, not knowing what to do next.

"My Lord, Norma must really be something," Jack said.

Claire shrugged. "Amy used to have terrible nightmares about Norma taking her away from me. It was much worse for her living with Norma than it was for me. I had my memories. . . ." Her voice trailed off. Jack shook his head.

"Norma had her convinced she was a hateful little girl. Amy used to apologize for everything, even if it was for something someone else had done wrong. And then there was the remedial classes thing." Claire swallowed. "But you know, I feel sorry for Norma. She didn't want children, but she took us in because my father had once asked her to."

Jack's two large hands enfolded Claire's. He brought them to his lips and kissed them. "If I ever run into that woman, I'm going to feed her to the coyotes," he said levelly. "No one should abuse kids and be allowed to get away with it."

"Oh, Jack, she never hit us."

"But she hurt you nonetheless. And I won't stand for that, ever." He touched her cheek. "Ever."

She stared at him, her eyes misting. Her heart went out to him, and yet Amy's case of nerves had reminded her where her loyalties and her future lay. A man like Jack could come later, but for now she had to be there for Amy as she had promised.

"No one will ever hurt you if I can prevent it," he went on.

Her throat tightened, but she forced herself to say what needed to be said. "Then you must keep away from me."

His lips parted in surprise. "Claire—"

"Please. I mean it." She raised her chin, tilting back her head to meet his gaze. There was pain in his eyes, and hurt, too, and she wanted to throw her arms around him and ask him to wait for her. In a year she could come back, or two, or maybe three. . . . "I'm all she has."

"Mistress Claire!" Have we yet more scarlet pillows?" Amy called.

Jack grabbed Claire's arm. "Dammit, it's not right! You two can't just cling to each other like shipwreck survivors."

Tears stung her eyes. "Please, Jack. It's right for *us*. We've been through so much. Don't make it even harder."

"Mistress! The pillows, have we more?"

"Aye, beneath the table," Claire said in a strangled voice, crouching down to locate the boxes hidden by the lacy tablecloth. Her hands were trembling as she dug through the merchandise.

I didn't mean that, I didn't, she thought wildly. *I don't want him to leave me alone. I want him beside me every minute I'm here.*

She rose. "Jack," she began, then caught her breath.

He was gone.

Amy nudged Claire in the ribs. "I always wondered where the word *stud* came from," she whispered.

In spite of her nervousness Claire rolled her eyes. "Try to compose yourself. This is a natural process."

Amy snorted. "I don't see anything natural about it."

Frankly neither did Claire. Their parents had done a piece about breeding Thoroughbreds in Kentucky, but it was another matter entirely to see the process firsthand. She was rather shocked by what she was observing: a mare, bound so that she couldn't so much as bob her head, standing in a tiny pen, padded with heavy protection to keep the stud from accidentally damaging her. At the moment the "teaser" stallion was being led to her. The poor horse's lot in life was to excite the mare and make her ready to receive the stud. Once that was accomplished, the teaser was led away to mate with a noncommercial mare—if he was lucky.

"Okay, bring him closer. Easy, now," Jack said, directing the men who held the teaser. The mare whinnied. "Oh, she's getting the idea now," he added, and the men laughed.

"This is pretty hotcha-hotcha," Amy said. "I'm getting embarrassed."

"Me too," Claire confessed. She considered flicking Nieve's reigns again and fleeing. Three long days had dragged by since she'd last seen Jack. Since their conversation on the opening day of the fair, he had taken her at her word and kept his distance.

She was dismayed by how much she missed him. Everything within her told her that if it was this painful now, it would be much worse later on. But she wasn't sleeping. Her once glove-tight gowns were hanging on her because she couldn't eat. Even loyal Amy, who never saw any of her sister's faults, was beginning to comment on her haggard look.

Finally, unable to bear it any longer, Claire had fidgeted through the afternoon, helped Amy close the booth, and, still dressed in her royal blue Elizabethan gown, mounted Nieve. If she could just see him from a distance, she'd told herself, it would be enough. She wouldn't speak to him or let him see her. She would only watch him as he moved through the bittersweet hour of dusk, lord of all he surveyed, unconsciously regal, incredibly handsome. It would be enough.

But Amy had foiled her plans. As Claire loped out of the camp Amy followed after her on Pajaro. Now the two of them sat sidesaddle on their horses, blushing, wondering what to do next.

"Maybe we should come back later," Claire murmured, grateful that Jack had not yet seen them.

"But we came all this way," Amy protested. "Besides, I told Lord P. S. we wouldn't be there for dinner."

"Oh, Amy. Jack didn't invite us!"

Amy grinned slyly. "But he will."

Claire picked up the reins. "But I wasn't even going to let Jack—"

"Hi, Jack!" Amy cried, waving vigorously. "It's us!"

Jack raised his head at the cheery greeting. His shoulders hunched in surprise and wonder. In her magnificent clothes Claire sparkled like an exotic jewel. He realized Amy rode beside her, but his eyes were drawn to Claire, and his heart clutched at the thought that at last she had come to him.

It was Karen who had told him to honor Claire's request. "Give her some space," his sister had advised. "When she's ready to be with you, she'll let you know."

Are you ready, my love? he asked silently as Claire slowly came toward him.

Amy, on the other hand, cantered up with reckless abandon and leaped off Pajaro, catching up the reins and stuffing them into Jack's hand.

"Hi," she said, grinning. "Are we interrupting?"

"Of course not." Over her head he watched Claire move closer.

At last she was near enough to greet him. "Hi." Her voice was so sweet and gentle, it made his breath catch in his lungs.

"God gi' good den."

She inclined her head. " 'Tis a good den."

He held out his arms. She bent from her perch on the saddle and flowed into them. Jack shut his eyes against the overwhelming tide of emotion that engulfed him as he touched her, breathed in her rosebud scent, savored her rush of breath on the center of his chest.

"My lady," he whispered for her ears only. His fingers on her hair were so light, it was as if he were caressing her aura. He felt her energy more than her physical being, and felt within himself the wanting, the hunger, the relief.

The desire.

Thank goodness you came, he thought, but already the elation of reunion was clouded by the fear that she would dart away again, disappear like an enchanted princess with the last ray of the sun. And yet he could feel her trembling in his embrace. He knew that holding him was arousing her. If it weren't for Amy, he thought, and for a moment he bitterly resented Amy and all the promises Claire had made to her.

"Uh, 'scuse me, Jack, but this ol' lady's rarin' to go," one of the hands said.

Claire immediately stepped back, breaking contact. On her face was a complex mixture of emotions that gave him hope and depressed him at the same time.

"I don't think this will take long," he said. He gestured to one of the men. "George, will you tell Consuelo there'll be two more for dinner?"

"I'll do it," Amy blurted out. She was beet-red, her eyes trained on the ground and not on the horses in the pen.

"Thank you," Jack said, hiding his smile at her shyness. How could he resent such a dear child?

As soon as he'd spoken she took off in a hurry. Jack raised a sardonic brow at Claire. "Anybody else want to abandon ship?"

But Claire wasn't listening to him. She was holding on to the padded metal pen, stroking the mare's forelock with a sure hand.

A cowboy named Todd McGregor held up a hand. "Pardon, miss, but you don't want to stand so close. Things could get a mite rough."

"I'm sorry," she said quietly, obeying him.

"You're from that fair, aren't you?" McGregor continued, giving her an appreciative once-over.

Jack frowned and said, "All right, boys, let's get this finished."

"It's been too hot all day for them to do it. Mate, I

mean," McGregor explained. Claire nodded. "Cool enough now."

"McGregor, can the chatter," Jack growled.

They led the chestnut stallion in. Jack felt a rush of pride as the magnificent creature threw back his head and neighed. His black mane bristled, and he stomped the ground with large, heavy hooves. In spite of the padding and the ropes, the mare fought as she sensed the presence of the other horse behind her. Snorting, the stallion reared onto his hind hooves, towering above the cowboys who worked to hold him.

There was raw power in the air, the straining and struggling of hundreds of pounds of horseflesh. The stallion was impatient, the mare unyielding.

The mare could be forced. But Jack nursed a superstition that rejection on the part of the animal decreased the chances of a successful impregnation. He knew his belief wasn't very scientific—there was plenty of literature that proved him wrong—but so far his breeding methods had produced prize foals. He saw no need to alter them if he didn't have to.

"Maybe we should wait," he said reluctantly. "We can try—"

Suddenly the mare stopped struggling. She stood docile and accepting, as if feeling the power and splendor of the male horse chosen to sire her foal. Her superior blood lines evident in the lines of her stance, she flicked her tail in a gesture of receptivity.

Then the stallion raised up behind her, assisted by the many cowboys on either side of his huge body, and took the mare. The horses' withers shook and they drew back their muzzles from their teeth, grimacing like humans in the throes of primal coupling.

To Jack it was a beautiful sight—two perfect horses uniting to produce a third. To him the miracle of creation was a profound experience. And he knew suddenly, fiercely, that the highest act of his life would be giving his seed to a woman he cherished in hopes of making a child together.

Claire, he cried out soundlessly, *oh, Claire.*

She was riveted to the earth, watching the mating as if she were in a trance. Her hands were clenched into fists at her sides and her breasts rose with her deep breathing. Where he had feared he would see repugnance, her features revealed the same exultation that had gathered inside him. She understood.

He couldn't stop looking at her. The sun, threatening to drop behind the mountains, cast her hair in bronze. Dusky pink tinted her cheeks and forehead. She was the most beautiful thing he had ever seen, more magnificent than his stallions, more precious than anything or anyone he could imagine.

Without speaking he moved to her side and caught her hand. Lacing his fingers through hers, he squeezed them tightly. To his joy, she squeezed back.

When their gazes met and locked he spoke to her with his eyes.

Tonight, his look said.

And hers answered, *yes.*

Once the mare was bred, the stallion was led back to his stable. With no distractions between her and Jack but her own fears and desires, Claire let him lead her to the house.

"I've missed you," he said simply. "I wanted to come to you so many times."

"I . . ." She faltered. *I don't know what I'm doing here,* she thought. But she did know.

Jack put an arm around her. "We'll talk later."

Too soon they were inside the cool white foyer. Amy burst in, trilling, "You've got company!"

Jack snapped his fingers. "That's right. The Hawthorns. I invited them before—" He glanced at Claire. "I invited them the morning the fair opened. Thought you two would like to meet them."

"He's a history professor. They know all about England!" Amy cried. "They've been there *five* times!"

"Imagine," Claire said faintly.

"He said my gown is authentic." She swept a curtsy in her low-cut costume.

"Well, that's nice," Claire said as they walked into the living room, "but I feel kind of silly meeting anybody while I'm dressed like this."

"That's how we met Jack," Amy told her. "Dr. Hawthorn wants to see our unicorn too."

Claire sighed. "He's really just a goat."

Both Amy and Jack looked at her as if she'd said something unexpected. A moment of silence passed, and then their attention turned to the Hawthorns as the couple walked into the room.

The professor was a mild, rotund man who smoked a pipe. "Well, well," he said, shaking Claire's hand. "Here's young Mary, Queen of Scots. Except, of course, that dear lady was over six feet tall."

"Yes, you do resemble her," Mrs. Hawthorn supplied. "Jack's been intriguing us with stories about you both." She smiled, first at Jack and then at Claire. "You certainly lead an interesting life."

"The best," Amy said. "We wouldn't have it any other way, would we, Claire?"

"Oh, no, of course not," Claire answered brightly, forcing a smile that apparently convinced the others. Amy nodded with satisfaction and the Hawthorns smiled. And Jack glowered.

The five of them sat in the living room, watching the sun go down and sipping margaritas. Despite Claire's sisterly frowns, Amy was drinking one, too, though not very enthusiastically. She licked at the salt rimming the glass like a kitten at a bowl of cream, Claire mused.

"It seems incongruous to be sitting in a Mexican-style ranch house sipping tequila with two Elizabethan ladies," Dr. Hawthorn said as he puffed on his pipe. "Very pretty ladies, I might add."

"By my troth, thou art full wanton," Amy said.

Dr. Hawthorn shook his head. "And clever ones too."

"Did you make your costumes yourselves?" Mrs. Hawthorn asked.

"Amy designed them. She's very good," Claire added.

Mrs. Hawthorn touched her husband on the shoulder. "We should take them to the exhibition, Dick."

He nodded. "It's at San Diego State, where I teach. The drama department has a display of forty years of costumes from student productions. Would you like to go?"

"Sure!" Amy cried. "When? Now?"

The professor laughed. "Well, how about after dinner?"

"Great!" Then she grimaced. "I mean, we can go, can't we, Claire?"

Claire could feel Jack's eyes on her, willing her to refuse. "Yes," she said breathlessly. "It sounds fascinating."

Consuelo appeared in the doorway. "Señor, dinner is ready."

"Mistress?" Jack said, rising and taking Claire's hand.

"We'll have to change our clothes," Amy said to Mrs. Hawthorn.

"I think Karen's got some jeans and things here that'll fit you," Jack told her. He brushed Claire's cheek. "You're not going," he whispered. She didn't respond as she sank into the chair he pulled out for her.

His eyes were on her all through the dinner of tacos, enchiladas, and other California-Mexican delicacies. Neither spoke. Amy filled the void with chatter directed at the two visitors.

"And what's London like in the summer?"

"Oh, lovely," Mrs. Hawthorn said, sighing. "You know, they have a wonderful costume institute in Bath. There's a fabulous museum there too. They have the bridal gown of Lord Byron's unfortunate wife."

"Really!"

"You're not eating," Jack said to Claire. He covered her hand. "Would you like something else?"

Shaking her head, she lifted her wineglass and sipped the dry burgundy.

"Don't be nervous, sweet," he murmured.

She set the glass down firmly. "What have I got to be nervous about?"

"Don't go with them."

Claire and I believe we lived before, in the Elizabethan age," Amy was telling the Hawthorns. "I mean, we're so *into* it. And we're so close too. It's like we read each other's minds."

"That must be special, to have a relationship like that," Mrs. Hawthorn commented.

"Oh, it is," Amy assured her. She laughed. "I don't think you can get much closer."

They finished dinner and dessert. No one seemed to notice that both Jack and Claire had fallen completely silent.

"Well, that was delicious," Dr. Hawthorn said, lighting his pipe. "But if we're going to that exhibition, we'd better hurry."

"Jack, can you show us where to change?" Amy asked, her eyes glittering with excitement.

He paused. Claire felt the pressure of his will on her. She hadn't planned for this to happen. She had only thought to watch him from a safe distance, then escape back into her life with Amy.

Safe. Love between her and Amy was safe. Everything else was transitory, dangerous. To be left behind as she explored the world . . .

No!

Jack rose and said, "Sure, Amy. Karen has a chest of clothes in the nursery. Come on." He pushed back his chair and began to leave the room.

"Cunk, let's go!" Amy sang out.

Claire took another sip of wine. Wrapping her

ngers around the stem of the glass, she raised her
ɿin and said, "I've got a little headache, honey. Go
head without me."

Jack turned in the doorway and looked at her.
is eyes filled with flame and his lips parted. Claire
ad a sharp vision of his expression during the
orses' mating, and heat painted her cheeks. She
ouldn't meet his gaze.

"Oh, I can't go without you!" Amy wailed. "Are
ou sick?"

"I—I'll be fine," she said unsteadily. "Please,
my, go ahead. Maybe I can go another night." *Lord,*
he thought, *I'm lying to her. Worrying her so that I*
an be with Jack . . .

"I'll take you," Jack said, showing Amy where to
o.

I'll take you. Claire shivered with mingled fear
nd desire at Jack's words. Then she exhaled deeply
nd rose from her chair. "All right," she murmured.

Six

Wearing a baggy jeans skirt and a turquoise-and-black-striped T-shirt yards too big, Amy hovered by the door of the Hawthorns' Volvo.

"You're sure you'll be all right?" she asked Claire.

Claire nodded. "Jack will trailer the horses back to camp," she said, aware of his shadow covering her as he stood in the beams of the dying sun. "I'll . . . get a ride with him."

"I wish you felt better."

Claire patted Amy's shoulder. "I'll be fine. I think I'm just tired."

"I can see why. You sure haven't been sleeping much."

Claire made a face. "I'm sorry if I've been keeping you awake."

"No biggee," Amy assured her. Her brown eyes crinkled. "After all, I'm younger. I don't need as much sleep."

Claire gave her a mock punch. "Wrong, kid. The older you are, the less you need."

"Then that's it, Cunky. You've just been aging at night."

"Begone, thou wretched child." Claire pointed at the Volvo and narrowed her eyes in a theatrically

tern expression. "How sharper than a serpent's
ooth it is to have a thankless sister!"

Chuckling, Amy curtsied. "As thou wishest, old
ne." She opened the door and climbed in.

"How long will you be gone?" Jack asked.

Any didn't seem surprised that he and not Claire
ad asked the question.

Mrs. Hawthorn rolled down her window. "Actu-
lly we were thinking of asking Amy if she'd like to
pend the night. I understand they don't have a
hower or bath in their trailer."

"We do have a sink," Claire replied defensively.

"That'd be fine," Jack cut in. "If Amy wants to."

"Oh, neat!" Amy cried. "Gosh, thanks!"

"It's settled, then," Mrs. Hawthorn said. "We'll
ring her back before the fair opens tomorrow."

They drove away. Feeling cast adrift, Claire
atched the car grow smaller, then disappear. She
as alone with Jack. She took a deep breath and
rned around.

"Jack, it's not your place to give Amy permission
do things."

His eyes were patient, but his jaw was firm. "It
asn't Amy I was giving permission to. It was you,"
e replied, and swept her up into her arms. Her royal
lue skirts billowed around her and draped over his
ody like the tail of an exotic peacock. With one arm
round her back and one under her knees, he carried
er toward the house.

"Jack," she breathed. "Jack, please."

The square bodice lifted and compressed her
reasts until the creamy globes threatened to escape
heir velvet prison. His breath on them was like the
ot Santa Ana winds, she thought, like firebrands.
eat rose inside her, filling her chest and abdomen,
nning embers that had smoldered since the first
ouch, the first phantom kiss in Karen's garden. He
ad seen her body then, examined her so intimately.
e had taken possession of her long before this
ight. But she hadn't yielded to his claim.

Until tonight.

"Jack, Consuelo—"

"Everybody's gone," he said, stepping across th threshold. "Consuelo won't be back until breakfast. He shut the door with the heel of his boot and kep walking. His grip was viselike as he climbed the tile stairs. The tap of his heels was slow, steady implacable.

"Jack . . ."

He was taking her to his bedroom. In her min she saw the huge brass bed and the skylight above and Jack's naked shoulders as he moved over her making love to her.

She stiffened. "Please, I'm . . ." *Afraid*, sh wanted to say. But the words she did manage to utte were lost in the noise of his boots on the wooden floo of his office.

Then he threw open the door to his bedroom an stood in the doorway.

It was as she remembered it, but blazing now i the sunset. Brilliant scarlet and burnt orang streaked the walls, reflected like searing flames in th mirrors above the dresser and washstand. She sav her own reflection, her blue eyes too big for her pal face, framed by tousled hair that fell like a curtai over her shoulder. The bed gleamed like a beacon and Claire caught her breath at the sight of it remembering the sensations he'd elicited in her th first time they'd lain on it together, the delirium tha had engulfed her. The abandon.

But Jack didn't enter the room. Instead, h looked down at her with infinite tenderness and said "Claire, I wouldn't hurt you for the world."

"I know," she whispered.

He nuzzled her cheek with his nose, moanin softly in his throat, his fingers digging into her flesh "Have you been hurt too much?" he asked. "Is ther enough love left in the world to heal all the wrong that have been done to you? All the unfairness? With his satiny lips he kissed the side of her mouth

"I can't comprehend the tragedy of your childhood. Nothing bad—really bad—has ever happened to me."

"I thank the Lord for that," she said, her voice breaking.

Tentatively she touched his face, absorbing the texture of smooth skin and masculine stubble, tracing the muscle and bone beneath. All of him, every part of him, was so dear to her.

He combed her hair with his fingers and murmured, "shh, shh," as if she were a troubled child who'd pressed her cheek against his chest. The coarse stubble at his throat tickled her forehead and her ear was filled with the thunder of his heartbeat. She closed her eyes and held fast to him.

After a few seconds he began slowly to rock her, back and forth, weaving strands of caring and protectiveness around her. The rocking continued. When she opened her eyes she saw that he had carried her back through the office and was heading for another part of the house.

He paused by the music room, as if searching for something, then shook his head and went down the stairs. Setting her down, he brought her hand to his mouth and kissed each fingertip, then shepherded her into the kitchen.

From a tiled pantry he took a dusty bottle of brandy, two glasses, and a small box covered in gold paper. He put them into a bag, along with a candle in a blue and white glazed holder and a box of matches.

He raided the linen closet next, running a hand over several plaid blankets until he chose one woven in kelly green and navy blue. Slinging it over his shoulder, he entwined his fingers with Claire's again and together they left the house.

Crickets sawed in the distance. Claire heard the mournful howl of a coyote and the soft nickering of the horses as she and Jack neared the stables. The night was hushed. A ring of clouds cradled the moon like a pearl set in silver.

"Would you hold the sack for a minute, love?"

Jack asked, handing it to her. He unlatched the double doors of one of the stables and flicked on a light, grabbing a lead rope from a line of tack on the wall.

The smell of fresh hay wafted from the nearest stall, where Nieve stood as if she'd been waiting for them. She tilted her head and nudged Jack's pocket when he led her out and slipped the rope over her head.

He took the bag, then lifted Claire and set her on the horse's bare back.

He regarded her for a moment, eyes sweeping up and down her body. "I can't get over how beautiful you are. Your eyes are as blue as midnight and your hair . . ." He trailed off, wrapping the lead rope around his wrist. "Let's go, Nieve," he ordered.

Though she was surprised, Claire didn't ask him where they were going. Instead, she gave herself over to the rhythms of the horse and the shifting patterns of the moon-shadows as they ruffled Jack's dark brown hair. He walked beside her, one long arm resting on Nieve's neck, occasionally stroking the horse's mane. Against his skin the half-moons of his well-trimmed nails were ivory, and she studied them as they journeyed up and down the mane, and close to her own thigh.

They walked for a long time. Though the direction was new, the land was much the same as the rest of Julian—fragrant pines and rolling hills, and the pervasive scent of ripening fruit. She'd been there such a short time, Claire thought, and yet it all seemed so familiar. As if she'd been there all her life.

She raised her face to the brilliant clusters of stars. *How can all this have happened so fast?* she demanded silently. *I don't understand it. I can't have fallen in love with a man I barely know. And my relationship with Amy—so quickly I've learned to keep things from her. I've distanced myself from her. For his sake.*

Her ears filled with a low, almost subliminal rushing. It took her a moment to realize that it was the sound of moving water. As Jack parted some manzanita bushes she leaned forward to drink in the fairy-tale setting he revealed.

From a granite precipice a sparkling waterfall cascaded into a pool below. Lacy trees like willows undulated around the perimeter, sheltering tall reeds from the moonlight. And there were flowers, huge bunches of them, fanned above wild grass.

"Oh, Jack, how lovely."

He helped her down. "Your fairy bower, fairy queen," he said, his eyes shining. "Come."

He tied Nieve's rope to a tree, then helped Claire down a stony incline that ended beside the pool. The balmy night air carried the mist from the waterfall back into the sky, frosting it with moonlight.

He slung the blanket off his shoulder and spread it on the ground, then held out his hand. "Come," he said again, and when Claire took it he sank to the ground, pulling her with him.

They sat facing each other, hands clasped almost formally, breath and thoughts swirling. Smiling, Jack opened the bag and brought out the candle, which he positioned on a rock and then lit. Its luster glowed on his face, refining the facets of his features, polishing the gold in his eyes.

What was he thinking? Claire asked silently. What did he hope for in his life, what was important?

Was she important?

Did he love her?

"Sing to me," he said. She looked at him. "Please. I love the sound of your voice."

Ordinarily she would have refused, feeling awkward and silly. But this was not an ordinary night, and he was not an ordinary man.

> " 'To-morrow is Saint Valentine's Day.
> All in the morning betime . . .' "

While she sang he poured two glasses of brandy

and sipped from one, leaning against the rock the candle was perched on.

> " 'And I a maid at your window,
> To be your Valentine.' "

As she finished he sat up and saluted her with his glass. "Thank you, valentine."

She flushed. "You're welcome. That was Shakespeare."

"Yes, I know. Ophelia's song in *Hamlet.*"

"Yes." She was surprised he knew, considering the fun he'd made of the old English they spoke at the fair. Maybe they'd been saying it wrong, she thought, and he was mocking them. But no, Jack was not a mocking type. He might tease, but he would never ridicule.

Still musing, she took a sip of the fiery liqueur, inhaling the vapor as it trickled down her throat. "Ah, that's good."

"It's old. My father bought it when I was born. Traded a prize-winning Hereford for three bottles."

She smiled. "He must love you very much."

"Yes, he does. My happiness—and Karen's—mean the world to him." He said it simply and with conviction, and Claire found herself forming a mental image of the wonderful man his father must be.

"My parents loved us, too, but it was hard for them to deal with kids. They were used to doing whatever they wanted whenever they wanted." She took another luxurious swallow of brandy. "That's difficult to do when you have babies."

Jack didn't reply. He lowered his head and swirled his brandy. When he finally raised his head she saw traces of anger in the set of his jaw.

"But they were good to us," she added quickly. "They loved us."

"Mmm." Putting down his glass, he shaped his hands around her face, tilting it toward the candlelight. His eyes darkened. She began to fall into them.

The world whirled in a circle like a hurricane, and his eyes were the calm center of the storm, the safe haven.

Safe.

"It occurs to me," he said, "that no one has ever loved you enough."

She swallowed hard, clinging to his gaze. Like the galloping of horses' hooves she could hear the advancing of this night's magic, and their mutual surrender to it. She could hear their cries of passion as surely as if they were making love right then. She could hear Jack calling her name in the throes of ecstasy. *Claire, oh my Claire, oh my love.*

"Amy loves me," she said shakily.

"You know what I mean. No man has ever cared enough—"

"No." She shook her head, trying to block out both his words and the echoes of his imaginary cries. "No, Jack, you're wrong." She picked up her glass and held it with both hands. "You're not the first man to come along, you know," she went on, her laugh sounding bitter in her own ears. "I mean, I'm not exactly . . . exactly . . ."

"Am I wrong?" He took the glass out of her tight grip and set it on the rock. "You've had sex before, but have you had love? Some other man has wanted you, but has he cherished you?" His voice dropped to a hoarse whisper. "Has he loved you the way I do?"

He stopped speaking, as if waiting for her answer. When she made no reply he took her hands and set them on his waist. Then he placed one hand behind her head and the other over the base of her neck and kissed her.

The contact was like an electrical shock that made her gasp, grabbing onto his belt as her lips parted in surprise. It was different every time. He was different, Claire thought, all the words running together as his mouth pressed against hers. Her body tingled as if he were touching her everywhere at once—her breasts and thighs and the small of her back. The core of her femininity quickened and pulsated with ancient forces that galvanized her with desire.

Jack penetrated her mouth. His tongue found and claimed hers. She was filled with his brandy taste. All her senses were filled with him, with the mingled scents of man and leather and pine, with the tender roughness of his fingers on her neck, with the corded strength of his muscles as he crushed her against him, entwining himself around her like a human vortex of passion.

He ended the kiss, then rained dozens more on her upturned face, gasping, "Claire, Claire," and molding his fingers beneath her chin. He kissed her hair, her ears, the bridge of her nose, returning over and over again to her lips. His hands were shaking. His voice was husky and deep, filled with an urgency that thrilled her and made the fires within her burn even brighter.

He caught up handfuls of her hair. She dropped her head back into his palm and gave a cry of pleasure as he ran his tongue down the arched column of her throat, then buried his face between her breasts.

Her back bowed like the curve of the moon, her breasts nearly exposed as they heaved inside the velvet bodice. Jack kissed them, running his tongue along the swelling curves, a leonine moan rumbling in his chest. Fingers did what lips did: He ran his nails over her creamy flesh, seeking the precious treasures of her nipples, captured within the tight gown.

"Oh, Claire, oh, my love," he murmured, echoing the cries of her fantasy. "Help me undress you. Let me see you lying naked in my arms beneath the stars."

It was happening, as she'd known it would. The barriers of self-protection were crumbling all around her, and yet she clung to the ruins, afraid, still not quite willing to open the doors herself. *If we make love, I will never forget him,* she thought. *He'll be in my heart for the rest of my life.*

Yet on hoofbeats the magic galloped closer. . . .

"Jack, stop," she whispered, gasping, but either he didn't hear or he ignored her as his trembling hands began unfastening the leather lacings that crisscrossed her spine. A cool rush of air caressed her bare skin as he eased the fabric apart.

"Jack, no." She tried to flatten her hands on his chest. "I—I've changed my mind."

"No, I see it in your eyes. You want me, my lady sweetheart, as much as I want you. You want to look at me, touch me, feel me inside you. Only you're afraid." He drew the velvet down her shoulders. The material stroked her breasts as it bunched around them, shielding them from his view. "Don't be afraid, Claire."

"I *am* afraid," she answered honestly.

"I know. But it's not a true fear, and we both know it. If you'll let me, I can make it fade. We'll go slowly. If it takes all night, we'll take all night." He spanned his long fingers over her chest. "Your heart's beating so fast, love. Like a hummingbird's wings."

His hair was as soft as rabbit fur as he lowered his head and kissed the side of her neck, her shoulders, the indentations of her collarbones. She couldn't help but touch him in return, and when she did her eyes flicked closed and her mouth grew slack. It was true: she did desire him. She wanted his hands, his lips on her, the hardness of his man's body inside her.

"I'm going to push your dress down now," he told her. "I'm going to caress your lovely breasts and kiss them."

He did as he said he would, pushing the gown to her waist. She blushed but did nothing to prevent him, as, inhaling sharply, he admired her. But he didn't touch her. He only looked at her as she sat barebreasted in the moonlight. Her forearms were still caught in the sleeves. She couldn't have covered herself if she had wanted to.

"They're the color of roses," Jack whispered. "I wonder if they're as soft as rose petals."

He sipped from his brandy glass, then offered it to her.

"My hands are stuck," she said shyly.

"Drink anyway." He held the glass to her lips. His elbow was almost brushing her breast, and Claire found herself willing him to touch it, touch her.

He set down the glass and pulled her arms from the sleeves, freeing them, and lifted her hands to his lips.

"My beautiful Mistress Claire. Rare, and so lovely." He smiled at her, then lowered his gaze to her breasts.

"Are they as soft as the petals of a flower?" he murmured, and filled his hands with them.

"Oh!" Claire cried as Jack touched her nipples. He centered the tingling points in his palms, circling the soft curves. "Proud and firm and yet like silk—"

"Jack, I'm embarrassed," Claire blurted out, and covered herself.

"No, don't be, sweetheart," he soothed her, gathering her in his arms. "What we're doing is part of nature, of life. Of love." He held her against his chest, shielding her from his own touch, and massaged her upper back.

"You're so tense," he observed, and set to melting the nervousness, working and kneading the flesh like clay. Three days of yearning for him had taken their toll. His deft fingers found tight knots of worry and sadness, then worked to loosen them until they no longer existed. He moved to her shoulders, asking, "Still sore?" when he reached the place she'd been hurt when she'd fallen in the garden.

In the crook of his neck she shook her head, sighing as he worked his spell. Her body began to relax against his, the firmness of his pectoral muscles a sensual contrast to her womanly form. A hypnotic lassitude combined with the growing, sure heat of uninhibited desire spread through her, and she put her arms around his neck, kissing him under his jaw.

"Oh, honey," he murmured, hugging her. She kissed him again.

"I'm okay now," she whispered.

His chuckle was warm and appreciative. "We have hours and hours, Claire. I wouldn't rush you for the world."

He gave her another hug, then settled her in the crook of his left arm, caressing her chest and the flat, smooth plane of her stomach.

"You look like a mermaid," Jack said, indicating the folds of the blue velvet billowing around her lower body. "A Lorelei, with long golden hair, singing beneath the waves."

She grinned at him. "Tempting sailors to their doom."

He nuzzled her, arranging her hair over her shoulders so that it cascaded over her breasts. "Well, you're definitely tempting me, woman." He caressed her skin with the lustrous curls, and Claire shivered with delight.

She covered his hand with hers and squeezed it. "And you're tempting me, man."

"I'm grateful for that, my love." He kissed her knuckles, then tasted each finger in turn. Little tingles skittered up her arm, sparking in her veins like static electricity. As Jack lifted her forefinger to his mouth, the moon shone on his hair, and Claire noticed for the first time the slightest sprinkling of gray at his temples.

I'm learning about him, she thought. *I'm getting to know little details—his sweet tooth, his love for his family, his warmth and patience. But there's so much more to know.*

And she had such a short time.

"What a sad look!" Jack said accusingly. "Did I cause that?"

She rested her head on his shoulder. "No. My mind just wandered for a second, that's all."

"We'll have to make sure that doesn't happen again."

His hand trailed down her stomach, then strained to pass underneath her tight waistband.

Chills eddied in Claire's loins as his fingertips brushed the top of her bikini underwear. Almost unconsciously she parted her legs a few inches, eager for the moment when he would touch her there, and set her ablaze.

But the dress was too tight for his passage. He snaked back out of it and sighed. Circling her navel with his thumb, he asked, "So, where's the secret zipper?"

" 'Zounds, milord, I dare not sew such a thing in mine raiment," she told him with mock sternness. "Lord Petit Sirrah would have my head." She raised herself up and began to undo a second set of lacings, concealed by an edging of gold braid studded with pearls.

Unbuttoning his shirt, Jack nodded appreciatively as Claire unthreaded the leather strips. With each movement they revealed more of their bodies to each other: her snowy, rounded hips, his bronzed, sinewy chest. Claire was fascinated by his male beauty, eager to run her hands along the undulations of his muscles, to learn the texture of the hair that swirled around his tiny nipples. When he took off his shirt she cupped his biceps in her hand, intrigued by the warmth of his skin, the feathery clump of hair under his arm.

"I love your touch," Jack said, running his chin along her arm. "I'm so aroused I can hardly stand it."

"Then let's . . ." she ventured, his words shooting through her. In her limited experience no man had been as patient or careful of her pleasure. She wanted to please Jack, both out of need and gratitude.

"Oh, no, not yet," he chided her. "Not until *both* of us are near the breaking point."

A rosy flush flared between her breasts and traveled up her neck, to glow on her cheeks. "I'm not sure I can reach that point."

He brushed her hair away from her forehead, an expression of infinite wisdom and tenderness lighting his face. "Oh, my sweet, how right I was. No one has cherished you properly." He traced her lips with his finger. "I don't care how long it takes, or *what* it takes, but I promise you, you'll reach that point tonight."

She lowered her head. "You won't get bored?"

He laughed gently and moved her onto his lap. The hard length of his arousal strained against his jeans. "Do you think I'm bored?"

"Not now, but—"

"Look what I brought," he said, supporting her as he leaned sideways and picked up the gold box.

She inhaled the voluptuous odor as he opened it. "Chocolate! I should have known it would be some kind of candy."

"Sweets for the sweet," he purred, selecting one with great relish and deliberation and holding it in front of her. "These are absolutely the best in the world. My mother buys them in a little French restaurant outside Tucson. I get a 'Care package' from her about once a month."

She understood what he was doing—changing the subject, taking off the pressure. Letting her know he really did have all the time in the world to make their first time together just perfect.

"Thank you," she breathed, allowing him to feed her the delicacy. It was buttery and sweet, and hid a surprise of a darker chocolate center flavored with a hint of mocha. It was so rich she didn't even have to chew it. It began to melt the moment she closed her mouth.

"Oh, that's wonderful," she said, talking behind her hand because her mouth was full.

Boyishly he nodded. "Isn't it?" He gobbled one up. "Pure heaven. Here, have another. I'm going to share my entire stash with you."

"Gosh, mister, you must really like me," she quipped, accepting a second tasty morsel filled with hazelnuts.

"Gosh, lady, I sure do." He sipped his brandy and she did the same. Sighing, he reached for a third chocolate and said, "Isn't this the good life? Eating bonbons and drinking aged brandy with a naked angel on your lap?"

Laughing, she hugged him. "You really know how to live!"

"Yes, I do." He grew serious. "And I know life isn't for being unhappy, or for making unnecessary sacrifices." She frowned and he stopped, exhaling deeply. "More chocolate, sweetheart?"

Ignoring his pointed remark, she didn't look at him as she plucked a piece of candy from the box.

He caught her chin between his thumb and forefinger and tilted her head back, forcing her to look at him.

"Hey," he said softly, "come back. Don't be angry."

Her blue eyes glittered. "I'm not angry."

"I have no business telling you how to run your life."

"Have some more chocolate," she urged him.

They ate more sweets and watched each other. They drank brandy. And Claire tried desperately to rally herself, crushed that the mood was spoiled.

"Hey," Jack said again in the same gentle tone, "I have something to show you."

A slow, wistful smile crept across her face. "What?"

"This."

He laid her on her back and kissed her deeply, passionately. It was a kiss that brooked no refusal, that would not accept anything less than her total response. His full lips stretched into a pale line as they crushed against her mouth. He inhaled sharply, his bare chest flattening her breasts, his arms rock-hard and unyielding as they enveloped her.

The ferocity of his advance shook her, destroying the pall that their discussion had cast over her. Gone were the defensiveness and hurt feelings. Gone, too, was her early mourning over their parting. As he urgently, almost brutally, aroused her she gave herself up to the moment, forsaking all else. Her back was taut, arching off the blanket, her arms wrapped around his neck. His hands dug into her sides as he kissed her neck, her shoulders, her stinging nipples, and her hair swept his forearms like a filigreed banner of satin.

"Claire, darling," he breathed, drawing down her dress and kissing her navel, the tops of her thighs, and placing a possessive hand over the magical triangle of yellow cornsilk. "Claire, blossom for me."

She became for him a hothouse flower—moist, ripe, pliant. Her body was sheened with perspiration, the center of her being opened like a velvet-petaled lily. Moving between her thighs, Jack laid claim to the fragile, dainty place, the pearly pink core of her womanhood.

"Oh, Jack!" she cried. Her body shuddered as a huge wave of pleasure overwhelmed her, hurtling tides of sensation through her. He caressed her intimately, slowly at first, moaning with approval as she responded to his actions.

"That's it, sweetheart, just let go. Let me hold you and please you. Tonight is only for you."

He increased his pace, and Claire writhed beneath his hand. "I'm ready, I'm ready," she murmured, unable to let go of her concern for him. She could feel her body gathering itself: Muscles tensed, blood roared in her ears. Strange and delicious sensations shot through her like falling stars, new feelings more intense than any she'd ever experienced before. It couldn't get any better than this, she thought. This was the best it could feel.

"Shhh, Claire," Jack said. "Don't think about me at all. Don't worry about my pleasure. If you want to make me happy, lie back and enjoy all the things I do.

Tell me what you like, and what you don't." He parted her legs and kissed her, his mouth on the tender places his hands had caressed. "Do you like that, love?"

"Ooh, yes," she moaned as her back arched off the blanket.

Raising his head, he drew his tongue up her body, pausing at each nipple. His hair was silky between her fingers as she ran them through it, feeling utterly consumed by the rapture he was creating.

"Please, now," she said hoarsely. "I want you so."

He sat back on his haunches as he unsnapped his jeans, eyes narrowed like a coyote sizing up its prey. He undressed with a deliberate slowness that was almost arrogant, obviously reveling in Claire's passionate torment.

Then he slid the jeans over his hips, taking with them his underwear, rising to his knees and then to his feet as he peeled them down his powerful thighs and long, muscular calves. He stepped out of them, towering over her. To Claire he looked like a god. Soon his perfect body would move on top of her, enter her, fill her. The realization moved her beyond words. She was filled with awe and a desperate yearning. Tears welled in her eyes and she held her arms open for him.

"Jack, I'm yours," she said throatily.

He sank between her legs. The moonlight illuminated moisture in the corner of his eyes as he regarded her. His face was radiant.

"*Are* you mine?"

"Oh, yes!"

"Will you do whatever I ask?"

She nodded, reaching out to touch him, but he moved out of her reach and wrapped his hands around her wrists.

"Then lie as still as you can for a little longer." He smiled. "You may think you're as aroused as you can be, but I know differently. You're a woman of rare passion, a treasure like fine wine. We have to let that passion breathe before you're ready for the drinking."

She gave a half-sob, half-laugh. "I feel as if I'm on fire."

His eyes grew hooded. "Soon, very soon, you will be."

What was love? What was it? Claire wondered, then let her mind slide into oblivion as Jack lay on top of her, his weight supported by his hands. He undulated over her, teasing her with love bites on her shoulders and upper arms. His velvety length prodded between her thighs and she opened them wider in an attempt to draw him into herself.

"Not yet," he whispered.

He kissed her. She forced open her flickering lids, gazing at the moon behind his naked shoulder. Jack's body was smooth as marble, scorching as lava. She wanted to explore it, make his body move to her touch as hers did for him.

She couldn't help marveling at his perfection. She raised her head to see the shape of his back, the muscles that ran diagonally down his spine to the tight, firm buttocks that flexed as he strained to rein in his passion. His nostrils flared as he breathed and his teeth were clenched, and suddenly the urgency of his desire flowed into her like a stream of molten steel.

Oh, Lord, I must have him, her soul demanded. *Please, please, please . . .*

With a cry she began running her hands along his body, as she had longed to, feeling his flat stomach, molding her fingers around his buttocks. Sliding beneath him, she found his nipples and sucked on them, clinging to him as he tried to move away. The buds contracted into two tiny points that she rubbed with her finger, thrilling to his gasps of pleasure. Then she trailed her lips down his stomach, following the swirls in the mat of hair, at last reaching the strength of his manhood. With a moan of triumph she stunned him with the intimate embrace.

"Ah!" Jack shouted. His cry echoed off the precipice before it was captured by the waterfall. His entire body shook in passion and she gloried in her power to excite him. *He's mine, he's mine,* she thought wildly. *I want to be everything to him. I want, I want . . .*

And then he pulled away, kneeling as he looked down at her. His shoulders were heaving and he was breathing hard. Tears streamed down his face and his eyes were blank, unfocused, lost in the dream they were sharing.

"Now," Jack said, his voice breaking as he prepared himself. "My love."

It was time. Claire threw back her head and parted her legs, offering herself to him.

He thrust himself into her with such power that she thought she would break in two. He was overwhelming, and she whimpered with the surprise and sheer ecstasy of it.

There were no more words, no thoughts. The world was Jack reaching into her with the heat of the sun and the beauty of the moon. With instincts eons old, Claire moved her body to his rhythm. They danced the ancient dance, sang the ancient song. They loved.

"Oh, Claire, oh, my love," Jack rasped. "Oh, my love, oh . . ."

His face was twisted into a grimace of exquisite agony. "Claire!" he cried, and loosed the ecstasy of his flesh into her.

She was engulfed by a pulsating white light that threw her into the sky. She lost herself and gained everything. She was one with the universe, hurtling through oblivion. Her body dissolved. She was so filled, she began to cry.

"Shh, shh," Jack soothed, kissing her. He pressed his lips against the crown of her head.

She embraced him, pulling him closer to her. Was it really she who had moved like that, cried out in passion? Who had excited this virile man until he wept with pleasure?

He rolled over and pulled her onto his chest. His heart was booming against his rib cage and she laid a protective hand over it, loving its vitality and health.

Claire closed her eyes, breathing in the smells of chocolate and brandy, the grass beneath the blanket and the scent of their lovemaking. Behind them the waterfall rushed on, and birds chirped in the trees. Farther on Nieve whinnied.

This is the finest moment of my life, Claire thought. *There has never been a moment more beautiful than this.*

She closed her eyes and held Jack tightly.

"Are you comfortable, love?" he asked, trailing his hand down her back.

She nodded. "Thank you."

"Oh, sweetheart, thank *you.*" He reached above his head and plucked a lavender flower. Brushing it against her cheek, he smiled. "Rest now," he told her. "We'll ride back in a while."

"I'm exhausted. But I feel so wonderful."

He hugged her. "It will always be like this for us, Claire. Forever and always."

Seven

Something was tickling her. Claire sighed in her sleep and scratched her ear.

There it was again. Yawning, she opened her eyes.

She was lying with her head in Jack's lap. Propped against the rock, he sat cross-legged, threading cream-colored daisies through her hair. When he saw that she'd awakened he smiled.

"Hello, angel."

He was naked, but he'd pulled his shirt over her to shield her from the night air. Holding it over her breasts, she slowly sat up, disoriented from her dreaming.

"Hi." She rubbed her eyes. One of the daisies dropped into his lap, covering him like the oak leaf on a classical statue. "I didn't mean to fall asleep! What time is it?"

"Does it matter?"

She considered. "I guess not."

"Time's stopped again for us." He pulled down the shirt and reached a hand over to her left breast. "Mmm, I love to touch you."

She inclined her head demurely. "I love to touch you too."

"Yeah, I noticed." He winked at her. "Boy, did I notice."

"I was having the strangest dream. About horses and fires and I was flying."

"Freud would have a field day with you." He picked up a flower and stroked the pale delta of her womanhood with the cool, satiny petals. Claire shivered and bit her lower lip, leaning against his chest. "So would I. So did I," he added. He draped the flower between her legs. "Was I in your dream?"

"Maybe," she said coyly. But he had been, as a great, thundering steed with eyes of flame. Even while dreaming she had recognized him.

"Do you believe in reincarnation?" she asked.

He shrugged. "I haven't thought much about it. I'm more concerned with the here and now. That stuff's just . . . stuff, as far as I'm concerned. There's no way to prove it one way or the other. So people might as well believe what makes them happy."

"Well, if it is true, then I think you were a horse once."

"Old Gray Jack."

"Oh, no. You might have belonged to a crusader. Or maybe even to the Earl of Leicester, Elizabeth's favorite."

His eyes twinkled. "They say Catherine the Great had an affair with a horse. Maybe that was me."

"Jack!"

He laughed. "I never could figure out how everybody who believes they've lived before has always been a king or a duchess. No one was ever just a serf or a pharmacist. Or," he added, grinning, "an old hoss thief."

"That's not true. Lots of people think they had ordinary past lives."

"I sure as hell never met one." He made a face. "It occurs to me that I'm stepping on your toes. Didn't Amy mention you two were into this?"

She moved her shoulders. "We've read about it."

"Tell me."

"Not now," she hedged. "It's a touchy subject." And too personal, she thought. This was something between Amy and her, and she felt disloyal talking about it with him. Already she'd stretched the bonds of trust between her and her sister. She could have just admitted to Amy that she was staying behind to be with Jack. Why the pretense?

Jack patted her stomach. "All right, we'll drop it. I really didn't mean to insult you, honey." He rose, pulling her up with him. "Let's go home."

"My home?"

He started to say something, then looked into her eyes and said, "I meant my place. Would you spend the night?" Before she could answer he added, "I'll take you back early." And Amy will never know, she knew he silently added.

"I'd like that." She slipped her hand into his. "Providing, of course, that you don't snore."

He widened his eyes with mock indignation. "Me? Mistress Claire, I would never be so gauche!"

"I'm not so sure about that."

"On the other hand, *you* have already proven just that gauche. I caught you in the act only minutes ago."

"No way, Master Youngblood. I have it on the highest authority that I am the perfect bedmate."

His mouth dropped open. "What?"

She looked down her nose at him, no mean feat since he was so much taller than she. "For your information, Amy snores. I don't."

He tapped her on her nose. "Well, you do."

"Don't."

"One of these nights I'm going to record you. Then you'll have to eat those words."

"Oh, yeah?"

"Yeah!"

He patted her bottom playfully. She jumped away, giggling, and balled her fists. "Oh, ya wanna play rough, friend? C'mon, put up your dukes!"

"Tsk, tsk. Such unladylike behavior. What would Queen Elizabeth say?"

Claire retained her fighter's stance. "Good Queen Bess could outdance, outdrink, and outswear most of her courtiers. She could probably outride *you* too."

"Ah, but could she outlast me?" He grinned sassily, planting his feet wide apart and jamming his hands on his hips. He was flaunting his nakedness, preening like a peacock, and Claire loved him for being so confident of himself.

"They say she died a virgin."

"Something you, thank goodness, will not do." He took an innocent step toward her. "C'mon, sweet. I want to show you something."

"Oh, I'll bet you do."

"No, really, it's over here." He began to walk away. Then, just as Claire lowered her arms, he whirled around and began to tickle her unmercifully.

"Stop! Stop!" she squealed, flailing at him as he attacked her stomach. "Jack, stop!"

They tumbled to the ground. Jack straddled her, holding both her wrists above her head, which left her underarms vulnerable for torment.

Her high, silvery laugh filled the air. "Enough!" she managed, thrashing. She kicked her legs but he avoided them, rising up on his knees.

"I'll get you back!" she promised, the last word dissolving into a crescendo of giggles. "I will!"

"Hah." He chucked her under the chin and released her, throwing his arms above his head like a rodeo cowboy finishing off a calf-roping.

Claire tried to sit up but she was too exhausted. Her abdominal muscles ached with laughter.

She looked at him wonderingly. She was like Amy around him, she thought. She got silly and giggly and flirtatious. She'd thought she was the serious, wary sister and Amy was the fun one.

Jack must have read her mind. "I like you like this," he said, helping her up. "You know, when we first met I thought your face would crack if you smiled."

"Thanks a lot."

"Well, it's true." He crouched down and peered at her through his heavy fringes of lashes. "Come on, baby. I want to go home and snuggle."

Home. She closed her eyes, savoring the word in all its bittersweetness. "Let's go."

Jack helped her on with her gown, though he didn't lace it up. Her underwear he put in the bag, along with the remnants of their feast. Then he dressed himself in his jeans and shirt, and pulled on his boots.

The horse was glad to be walking again, gladder still when she realized they were going back to the stable. When they arrived Jack put some more hay in her trough and gave her a hearty pat, then shut the stable doors and lifted Claire into his arms.

"The seduction of Claire, part two," he drawled.

"Aren't you too tired to carry me?" she asked delightedly as he retraced his path of the early evening, carrying her toward his bedroom.

"Naw. After all, you weigh only ten pounds more than Amy." He kissed her cheek. "And believe me, that ten pounds is definitely worth the extra effort."

"That's a compliment," she decided. "Thank you."

He bowed his head. "Master Jack, at thy *servicing.*"

They entered the bedroom. This time it was swaddled in the ebony blanket of night, and this time Claire smiled as they sank into the downy mattress.

Fingers moving like spiderlegs, Jack traveled under her skirts. "I'm coming back for more, Claire," he whispered in a theatrical tone.

"Okay," she whispered back.

He began to sing. " 'And when I get to heaven, I'm-a gonna kiss my woman's—' "

The phone rang, startling Claire. Jack rolled his eyes and continued up her inner thigh, muttering,

"It's those damn people overseas. They forget about the time difference when they call." He patted her. "I'm not going to answer. The answering machine in the office will get it."

"Maybe it's something important," she said, eyeing the phone.

"Nothing's more important than what I'm doing."

The machine clicked on. An official-sounding voice—not Jack's—explained that the offices of Rancho Espejo were closed for the day, and requested that the caller leave a message.

"It's Barbara Hawthorn," came the reply. "Jack, are you home by any chance? This is an emergency."

"Oh, my Lord!" Claire cried. She leaped forward and picked up the phone. "Mrs. Hawthorn? This is Claire van Teiler. Has something happened to Amy?"

Mrs. Hawthorn paused. "Well, yes, dear, I'm afraid something has. She asked me not to call, but that was out of the question. I guess Jack was out when I tried before. I left some messages."

"Oh, no!" She went ashen. Behind her Jack put a steadying hand on her shoulder. He gestured for the phone, but she clutched it, shaking her head.

Mrs. Hawthorn hesitated. "I don't know how it happened. One minute we were on the road and the next we weren't. At first we thought it was just the tire. It blew out, you see." She laughed weakly. "Your little sister changed it. Then I stayed with my husband while she went to flag down help. She fell down an incline and—"

"Oh, Amy !"

Jack's grip grew tighter. "What is it?"

Mrs. Hawthorn continued speaking. "Dear, she only broke her ankle. They're releasing her right now. We're at the hospital. My husband has a slight concussion."

"Oh, I'm so sorry. But Amy—" Faltering, she looked at Jack, who took the phone from her.

"Barbara?" He nodded as he listened. "Okay.

Good. A cast? Damn, a concussion? How's he feeling? Poor Dick. No, no, we'll come right away to pick you up."

He set the receiver in its cradle and took Claire in his arms. "Honey, it's all right. She only broke her ankle."

"Only!"

"She's going to be all right. They've X-rayed it and put a cast on. The doctor told her it would heal in no time."

Claire wrung her hands. "Mrs. Hawthorn said they've been trying to reach us."

"Yes, well, that couldn't be helped."

"But she was *hurt!* And I was . . . was . . ." She turned away from him.

"You were making love with me," he said. "Is that so terrible?"

She pressed her fist against her mouth. "She's all I have."

"Dammit! She is *not!*" Jack shouted. The fury in his voice shocked her so much that she rose from the bed. His eyes flashed. He held himself rigidly, as if willing himself to calm down. Finally he took a deep breath, held it, and let it out.

"I'm sorry, Claire," he said. "I was out of line. Let's find some clothes for you and get to the hospital."

"Thank you," she said, feeling wretched.

"I almost forgot. Amy didn't have her purse with her and the hospital wants some identification."

She couldn't look at him. She'd hurt him, and he'd frightened her with his anger. But he knew where she stood, she told herself. It wasn't as if she'd misrepresented her feelings.

"Her purse is in the van. We'll have to go to the camp."

He nodded. "You can change there, then. Let's go." As he stood he touched her arm. "Claire, I didn't mean to bark at you. Please forgive me."

She managed a sad smile. "I do. If you'll forgive me."

He fondled her earlobe. "Cunky, you did nothing that needs forgiveness."

Oh, yes, I did, she thought. *I fell in love with you.*

They drove to camp in a shiny black Mercedes station wagon. Hurriedly Claire threw on a sky blue skirt and a muslin blouse, found Amy's purse, and joined Jack back at the car.

Keith Mandell was with him. Both men turned at the sound of her footsteps. Jack's face was white, his eyes dark as the night.

"Hey, Claire," Keith greeted her. "I was just telling Jack the news."

She frowned. "What news?"

"Weren't you here for the meeting tonight? We're leaving early. Lord Petit Sirrah had a fight with the town council and we're cutting our date short. We're splitting next week." He sighed. "Too bad. Sue and I are moving a lot of glass."

Claire stared at Jack. "But won't he change his mind?" she asked evenly.

"No chance. He's already lined up a new date someplace in Los Angeles. Next to some dippy shopping center. I think it's crummy."

Her heart clutched. *Leaving!* So soon?

Too soon. She reeled. Leaving Jack. She'd known it would come to this, had known better than to try to force a lifetime of loving into four short weeks.

She had known it would break her heart.

Jack raised his chin. "Come on, Claire. We have to go."

Numbly she climbed into the car, holding Amy's purse like a shield. Jack slammed the door and stalked around to his side. When he turned on the engine he threw the gear into reverse with a vicious yank.

Tension seethed inside the car, choking Claire so that she could barely swallow.

Jack sighed. "Well, when it rains it pours, doesn't it?"

Claire didn't say anything, only nodded.

Claire didn't wait for Jack when they pulled into the hospital parking lot. She jumped from the car and ran to the emergency room entrance, her yellow hair flying.

Wearily Jack climbed out and shut the door. He was ashamed of himself for treating her badly, but, dammit, he had feelings too. Did she think it was easy to fall in love for the first time, and with a woman who was planning to ride off into the sunset without you in one damned week?

Hooking one hand through the door handle, he swore under his breath and slumped. He hurt. Why'd it have to be Claire anyhow, with all her problems and her awful childhood and that stranglehold she and her sister had on each other?

He blew his hair away from his forehead. He knew the answer. It had to be Claire because it couldn't have been anyone else.

He patted the Mercedes and stuck his hand into his pocket. After she left, he told himself, he'd go back to Jessie. He'd try to forget her in Jessie's arms and he'd never fall in love again.

But he wouldn't forget her. He knew it. He would never fall in love again because he would never stop loving Claire.

"And I won't give you up without a heck of a fight, fairy princess," he murmured, and headed for the emergency room.

What he found there surprised him. He'd expected to see the two sisters fondly embracing, Claire fussing over Amy, Amy tearful but putting on a brave face.

But the two of them sat uneasily facing each other, and the atmosphere in the room was as strained as it had been in the car.

"I'm sorry Jack wasn't there to answer his phone," Claire was saying.

"I told them not to call him," Amy replied. "But they wouldn't listen to me. They'd already phoned Karen."

"Well, they were right! How on earth were you going to get home?"

"Karen and Tom said they'd take me back."

A nurse sailed around the corner with a pair of crutches. "Here we go," she said cheerfully. "Can you stand up?"

Amy struggled to lift herself out of her chair. Claire moved to help her but Amy snapped, "Please, Cunky, I can do it." Claire looked as if Amy had slapped her.

Jack walked over to them and put a comforting hand on Amy's arm. "Hi, little sis. I hear you've been skiing down the Interstate."

She smiled wanly. "Hey, Jack. I'm sorry if they got you out of bed."

"No problem. That's what big brothers are for. And sisters," he added meaningfully.

She sighed. "I'm being a grouch, aren't I? Cunky, I'm sorry. It's just that . . ." She trailed off. "Now I can't dance in the court revels. Lord Petit Sirrah won't like that."

"He'll understand," Claire promised. Jack was moved by the look of relief on her face. Her sister's love meant so much to her. He understood that they had gone through a lot together. He understood, but still—

"Is that why you're so upset?" Claire asked.

Amy hesitated. A muscle jumped in her cheek. "Mmm-hmm."

"But that's nothing! In fact, it'll be kind of nice to have more time to sew, won't it?"

Jack watched the two of them. Amy was miserable, yet Claire wasn't fully aware of it. There was more going on here than Claire realized, and Amy apparently wasn't planning to tell her about it.

At least in public, he reminded himself. In front of him.

"Ladies," he said brightly, "your chariot awaits. May I take you to yon Gypsy camp?"

Amy sniffed. "Forsooth, milord, I'll have no truck with Gypsies!"

"Good. I didn't bring the truck and I left the Gypsies at home too."

"Oh, no, don't start punning again!" Claire wailed. She put an arm around Amy's shoulders. "Let's go, baby."

"Okay."

"I'd like to see Dick for a few minutes," Jack said. "I told Barbara we'd give her a lift home too."

"He's in a room down the hall," Amy said. "Just sneak past the nurse."

"Okay. Thanks. I'll only be a minute." He began to walk down the corridor.

"I almost forgot," Amy called. "Your sister's in there! Please say good-bye to her for me."

Jack lifted his hand to show he'd heard, then walked on.

Karen and Mrs. Hawthorn were hovering over the professor, who was sitting on an examination table. He was wearing a green paper gown and his bare feet dangled over the edge.

"I'm all right, I tell you," he growled. "It's just a bump."

"Now, Dick," said Mrs. Hawthorn, "they want to watch you."

"Mmph." Dr. Hawthorn was clearly annoyed.

"Greetings," Jack said cheerily. "Brother, what some people won't do for attention."

"Hi, Jack," the women chorused.

Jack gave his sister a peck on the cheek and put his arm around Mrs. Hawthorn. "Are you all right?"

"Just shaken." She ran a hand through her hair. "I'm afraid I fell apart when I saw Dick's bloody forehead. Amy took charge then. You know, she's a real trooper. She seems like a flighty little thing, but when push comes to shove, she's really on top of the situation."

"Amen," Dr. Hawthorn said. "Extremely bright too. We were talking to her about going to college. She seemed interested, but she kept insisting she didn't want to go for at least a couple of years."

"She says she's set on traveling," Mrs. Hawthorn put in. "But I wonder. On the way back from the costume display, before our little mishap," she said ruefully, "she was poring over a San Diego State catalogue I gave her." She sighed. "It seems like such a waste."

"Well, she's young yet," Dr. Hawthorn said.

"That's true." Mrs. Hawthorn smiled at Jack and Karen. "It was sweet of you all to drive down here in the middle of the night. Everybody's been such a help. Tom's off now, filling out those awful forms."

Karen peered at her brother. "Are *you* okay? You look a little peaked."

He shrugged. "I'm fine."

She flashed him a private look of disbelief and hooked her arm around his. "Barbara, you said you wanted a cup of coffee. Jack and I will go get it."

"I want one too," the professor insisted.

Mrs. Hawthorn patted her husband's cheek. "The doctor said 'no.' "

"Humph."

Jack and Karen walked into the hall, at the opposite end from where Claire and Amy waited. Jack glanced at the two sisters, heads bowed as they talked.

"It's Claire, isn't it," Karen said.

"I almost wish I could have both of them," he replied bitterly.

She gave him a squeeze. "Why do you say that?"

"Well, I hate to break up a matched pair."

"Are you sure you can? Break up the pair, I mean?"

He turned an anguished face to her and shook his head.

"Oh, sweetie," Karen murmured, stroking his chin. "I'm so sorry."

"They're leaving in a week. That lunatic leader of theirs quarreled with the town council."

Karen sighed. They reached the coffee machine and Jack fished in his jeans, producing two quarters. He thrust them into the coin slot and said, "She likes it with cream and sugar, right?"

"Yes. Jack—" She hesitated. "All this has happened so suddenly. You know, you've never cultivated a relationship with a woman before. Are you sure this is for real? If it's just an infatuation, you'll get over it." She tapped her fingers on his shoulder as the machine spewed steaming liquid into a paper cup. "Jessie was in today," she drawled, "wondering where you've been these past few days. She's a nice lady—"

"All she wants is my bod," he quipped, but his voice was sad.

"I'm not so sure about that. I think she's always said that because she didn't want to scare you off." She took the coffee from him and rose on tiptoe to kiss his cheek. "You're a pretty good catch, you know—rich, handsome, great with kids."

"Oh, lordy, I want to marry me myself."

"Jack, you sound so miserable." She laid her head against his chest. "Have you asked her to stay?"

"More or less. She's determined to travel with Amy. They dreamed about it for years, and I guess nothing's going to stop them now. But damn!" He turned away. "Let's go. I don't like to see grown men cry."

"Oh, Jackie, I know she cares about you. Don't give up."

He chewed his lower lip. "Well, I haven't yet. After all, I've still got seven whole days to convince her I'm worth giving up everything and everybody for."

"Amy could live here too."

"And do what? Marry Davey?"

She laughed. "Why not?"

"Because he's a knucklehead. Forgot to close the gate today and some dumb cow came for a visit."

"She could go to college."

Jack shrugged. "They keep saying they want to travel."

They turned back toward Dr. Hawthorn's room. He spoke again, his voice harsh. "No, this isn't the kind of life for them. They want to live in Never-Never-Land. Cabbages and kings. Paper dragons. Do you know they even believe in reincarnation?" He inclined his head and raised his brows in a pose of mock hauteur. "I mean, can you see me with a woman like that?" Before she could answer he took a sip of Mrs. Hawthorn's coffee. "This stuff is terrible. It's going to put Barbara in the hospital too."

Karen stood in front of him and put a hand on his chest. "I can always tell when you're upset because you start to joke like this. If there's anything I can do, you will let me know, won't you?"

Managing a smile, he touched her cheek. "You turned out pretty well for a bratty little sister." He dug in his pocket. "Want a jellybean, Silver Mouth?"

"Want a sock in the kisser, brother dear?"

Grinning, they embraced. "You've still got me," Karen whispered. "And everybody else who loves you."

"Yes, I know." The problem was, he wanted Claire.

" 'God save Their Royal Majesties
The Lord and Dame of May!
God 'ild them from unhappiness
and fill with joy each day!

Anon, ye nobles and ye folk!
Come the champions and the poor!
For whilst our Lord and Lady reign
'tis May forever more!' "

Claire shook her tambourine above her head and cheered with the rest of the royal procession as it wound through the village, but her heart was heavy.

Amy, sidelined with her broken ankle, looked terribly unhappy, and Claire was sure she knew why.

She was jealous of Jack. Claire could understand it. For so long it had been just the two of them, planning their freedom, dreaming of a new, exciting life free of Aunt Norma's influence. Jack had been right. Amy was not all Claire had. But Claire was all Amy had.

Amy's moping had begun the night of the accident, when it had come out that Claire had been at Jack's when Mrs. Hawthorn had called. Things between her and Jack had grown so serious that it must be apparent to everybody, she thought. Mrs. Hawthorn hadn't even been surprised when Claire answered Jack's phone.

Amy must feel terribly threatened, Claire mused as she dropped a curtsy and the Cunninghams swept by, resplendent in their golden capes and crowns. Claire herself was dressed in a beautiful velvet gown the color of sable, the sleeves slashed with black and white, and a gold and black stomacher running from below the waistline to the bodice. Her ruff was dotted with brown "jewels," the stiff lace repeated in a heart-shaped cap.

Amy had made all the clothes on their treadle sewing machine, from the first rough basting down to affixing the lacy cuffs on Claire's gloves. She had begun this particular costume three days before the accident and had finished it in the early morning of this, the second day after. Usually Amy was merry and excited when she worked on large projects, but since the accident she had become somber and taciturn—almost as if she and Claire had traded personalities.

Claire looked at her again. She was studying a book of some kind and she looked pale and tired. She'd been reading almost nonstop since the accident.

To shut me out, Claire thought dismally. Well,

soon they would move on and things would get back to normal.

Her heart lurched, but she resolutely willed away the panic that rushed over her at the thought of leaving. *Jack, oh, Jack, how can I bear it without you?* she cried inside. *How can I go on?*

" 'Tis May forever where we do dwell!" His Majesty proclaimed, mounting the dais where his throne glittered in the hot August sun. "Our subjects do live in joyous harmony!"

"Huzzah!" Claire cheered with the others, forcing tears away.

This was the life she'd chosen, she told herself. She wanted this life. She wanted to travel, never staying in one place.

You want to be safe, a tiny voice accused her. *You don't want anyone to hurt you again, ever. That isn't life. It's a fairy tale, as Jack said. You're forestalling the inevitable. Amy won't need you forever.*

"But she needs me now," Claire murmured aloud.

"Love and joy preside o'er our festivities!" Her Majesty added. "We are excellent blessed with the smile of Venus and the bounty of Bacchus!"

"Huzzah!"

"Let the revels begin!" the king demanded.

Claire joined the others in a circle around the maypole, darting a glance at Amy's wistful face. When Amy realized Claire was looking at her, she brightened and waved.

My sister, Claire thought lovingly. *My dear little one. She tries so hard.*

Colorful streamers hung from the tall pole, which was decorated with garlands, and Claire picked one up as she faced her partner, Old Tim the Cobbler. He wore a big leather apron over his simple clothing. They bowed to each other, a piper and a drummer began to play, and they danced the maypole dance.

She brushed shoulders with the others of the troupe—her friends, her companions in the past wonderful year—left, then right, left, then right, crisscrossing their banners until the entire company's streamers wove around the pole. Keith and Sue, Old Tim, Sir Goodwrench and his lady, who were the owners of Merlin—the familiar faces of her Gypsy family blurred past her. Yes, this was her life, she told herself resolutely, beginning to relax as the tune and the rhythm of the steps soothed her. She'd be okay without him.

And then she saw Jack watching with the rest of the crowd on the perimeter.

"Oh," she breathed, and ran into the person she was supposed to pass.

"Sorry," she mumbled, then did it again with the next person.

Her garland fell off her head and she caught it awkwardly. His mere look unnerved her. There was the feeling of being trapped and the desire to be trapped. She felt like the fawn in the forest, trembling before the towering horses and riders.

The dance mercifully ended. She bowed to Tim, who said, "Art thou ill?"

"Nay, Goodman Cobbler. 'Tis the heat."

"Aye, 'tis hot as Hades. Glad I shall be to move north."

"Aye."

The dancers trickled away, to return to their booths or mingle with the paying guests. In the crowd it was easy to elude Jack.

She sat beside Amy. "So, sister fair, how goeth thy day?"

Amy sighed. "Fine. Look, here cometh Lord P. S. with Merlin."

"Aye, right on time."

It was Claire's and Amy's turn to sit with Merlin, posing for the tourists, who paid a dollar for the privilege. During their shift someone else watched their booth for them.

Lord P. S. was leading the goat on a leash, batting him on the nose when the animal tried to eat his velvet cape.

"Beshrew ye, rogue! By my troth, thou art a cutpurse!"

"He be more than that, milord, he be an *eat*-purse," Amy retorted, taking Merlin's leash. "But I warrant we two shall handle him mightily."

"Aye, milady, I trowe you shall," Petit Sirrah replied. He smiled over their heads. "Ah, milord Jack! How fine a day 'tis, aye? Your lady awaits," he chirruped, and sailed away.

Amy looked at Claire. "*Are* you his lady?" she asked while Jack was still too far away to hear.

"Of course not." Claire laughed nervously. "I just wanted to have some fun, you know? Like you told me to."

Amy's face was unreadable. She flicked the little bell on Merlin's collar and fussed with arranging a circlet around his neck.

"A farthing for your thoughts," Claire murmured, touching her hand.

"I just can't wait to get out of here," Amy retorted. "I'm glad we're leaving early."

"Oh. I didn't know you didn't like it." Claire hoped she'd kept the surprise and hurt out of her voice.

Amy shrugged. "It's okay. I didn't mean it the way it sounded. It's just that . . ." She raised stricken eyes to Claire.

"Honey, what's wrong?" Claire leaned forward. "Is it something I've done? Have I hurt you?"

Amy took a deep breath. "Cunky, I really want to go to—"

"Hello," Jack said behind them.

"Howdy," Amy replied, but Claire said nothing.

He crouched beside Merlin and scratched him around his unicorn horn. "How're you two today?"

Amy flashed him a brilliant smile. "Passing fair, milord. And thou?"

"Fairly passable. Hey, Merlin, look what I brought." He put his hand in his pocket.

"No jellybeans," Amy warned.

He pulled out a red apple. Merlin lunged for it, sinking his sharp little teeth into the shiny skin.

"Haven't seen much of you two since the accident," Jack commented, looking at Claire.

"Chide us not. We have been busy."

"Too busy, then. Is there anything I can tempt you with to come on over to my place?"

"It will take more than apples," Amy riposted.

Jack's eyes didn't leave Claire's face. He was probing her. She could feel his intensity even when she looked away.

"Oh, I've got lots of other things beside apples," he replied. "I mean, how could any intelligent woman pass up a guy like me?"

"Gosh, I just don't know," Amy said, fluttering her eyelashes. "Do you, Claire?"

They both looked at her, Amy laughing, Jack masking his pain behind a pleasant smile. She swallowed.

"No, I don't know how anybody could pass you up," she said quietly.

Jack let the smile slip. "Glad to hear it."

But I'm going to, she added inwardly. *Oh, my darling, I'm going to.*

Eight

Jack talked with Claire and Amy while they posed with Merlin. To Claire the hour was like a small sip of water after two days in the desert. She'd thirsted for him, and the short hour he sat beside her was not enough to slake her craving. She watched him joke and chat with her sister and some of his neighbors who had turned out for the fair. Everyone liked him. He was charming and warm and seemed to know something about everything. It was a pleasure to observe him, to watch the sun glimmering on his hair, feel the energy pulsing through him. He was so full of life that it communicated itself to those around him—especially to Claire.

And then Jessie Reynolds appeared. The most striking thing about her was the mane of blond hair framing a heart-shaped face with electric green eyes. Clad in skintight jeans, a pastel plaid Western shirt, and alligator boots, she was the epitome of cowgirl glamor. When she walked over to Jack and laid a proprietary hand on his arm, a tourist snapped a picture of her.

"So this is where you've been hiding yourself!" she said. Her voice was husky, almost like a man's. Claire found herself making comparisons between herself and the woman. Earthy, voluptuous Jessie Reynolds was definitely more Jack's type than she.

Jack introduced everybody. "Jess owns the miniature horse ranch." He winked at Jessie. "We trespassed."

"The mini-neighs!" Amy cried. "Oh, I just love them! They're so *cute!*"

Jessie chuckled at Amy's enthusiasm. "I'm so glad you think so. Want to take one off my hands? I can give you a great deal."

Amy snorted. "It would have to be 'great' as in 'free.' "

"Besides," Claire added, "we wouldn't have anyplace to keep it."

"We travel light," Amy affirmed.

Yes, Claire thought. They even left their hearts behind if they got too burdensome.

Jessie turned to Jack. "Why don't you come for dinner some night? I'll make that ham you like so much."

Claire couldn't help her flash of jealousy. He wouldn't miss her at all, she thought hotly. In fact, it didn't look as if he had been lonesome before she'd showed up, either.

"That would be nice," Jack said vaguely.

Jessie drew lazy circles on the back of his hand. "You haven't had any lately. Ham, I mean." She smiled directly at Claire. "I'm a great . . . cook."

"So is Claire," Amy piped up. She flashed an engaging smile at Jessie. "I'd love to see those little horses again!"

Jessie shrugged. "Why not come over now?" Her invitation obviously included Jack.

"We have to relieve the people who are working the booth," Claire reminded her sister.

Amy slumped. "Darn. You're right."

"I'll help you," Jack interposed. "Go ahead with Jessie, Amy."

"Thanks!" She smiled at Jessie. "I just need to change my clothes, okay?"

Jessie was looking at Jack, appraising him. "Okay," she said, chuckling and shaking her head as she gave him a light punch on the arm. "Amy, I'll meet you at the exit in a few minutes." She sighed good-naturedly. "Well, Youngblood, see you later."

" 'Bye, Jess." He bent down and kissed her cheek.

Appreciative glances followed Jessie as she walked away. Claire studied her retreating figure, wondering what she meant to Jack. If they'd made love . . .

"She's just a friend," Jack said.

"She doesn't want to be," Claire replied.

"Correction: 'didn't.' She just threw in the towel. Or didn't you catch that?"

"I—"

"Lady Claire, we are returned," someone interrupted behind her. It was Sir Goodwrench and his lady. "We shall take on the watching of ye unicorn."

"As you will," Claire replied, curtsying. She looked at Jack. "Wert serious about helping in my booth?"

"Sure."

Her eyes twinkled and she forced herself not to grin. "Then we must needs hurry."

"As you will." He swept a bow that would have been the envy of Lord Petit Sirrah, then took her hand in his, swinging her arm as he began to walk toward the rows of booths.

She stopped. "Nay, good sir, first thou must change thy clothes."

"Huh?"

"Come with me to the van," she ordered imperiously. "You must have proper apparel."

He let her lead him over to the van. When she opened the door he paused on the threshold.

"I've missed you," he said softly, urgently.

She couldn't look at him. "Me . . . too."

"Then why have you been avoiding me?"

Swallowing, she brushed his wrist with her fingers. "Please don't ask, Jack. I'm going in five days. Let's leave it at that."

"No way."

"Jack, Amy's—" She sighed. "Amy's feeling threatened by you. I have to reassure her."

"Oh, and the best way to accomplish that is by smothering her with attention," he shot back. "Claire, she's grown-up now. You can stop worrying about her."

She struggled with herself, willing down the anger. He couldn't possibly understand. He'd grown up happy and secure. He didn't know what it was like to have the kind of childhood Amy had had. His impatience and lack of empathy were understandable, and yet—

"I have to go to a benefit tonight," Jack said, changing the subject. "I'd like you to go with me." She hesitated. "The Hawthorns are planning on asking both of you to spend the night with them, so Amy will have a place to go too." He brushed her hair away from her forehead. "Please, Claire. Do this for me."

Oh, she wanted to. But she knew it was wiser not to. "Take Jessie. She'd love to go."

He smiled. "Ah, you're jealous. That's terrific."

"I am not!"

"Oh, you wench, you. You're practically spitting fire." Kissing her nose, he laughed when she tried to jerk her head away. "Riles you up to think about her and me, doesn't it?"

"Not really."

"Claire, Jessie's a gracious lady. She knows when to bow out."

"Bow out? In five days she'll have you back and you'll—"

Just then Amy hobbled up, dressed in a jeans skirt and a muslin blouse, her yellow hair fluffed around her face like sunlit clouds. She'd tied blue and white ribbons onto her crutches to match her outfit. "Well, I'm off!" she announced. "How do I look?"

"Great, sweetie," Claire said.

"The Hawthorns are planning to invite you to dinner," Jack told her. "They're asking Claire, too, but I want her to go out with me instead."

Claire shot him a look, which he ignored. He was studying Amy, and gestured for Claire to do the same.

Her sister had the oddest expression on her face—pensive, wistful, and excited all at the same time. "I'd love to go," she said softly.

"Shall I go with you?" Claire asked.

Amy glanced at her cautiously before she replied. "No, it's okay. You go with Jack."

"If you'd rather—"

"No," Amy said firmly. "It's better—I mean, it's fine." She smiled at her sister. "Gotta go. Jessie's waiting for me."

She took off, scrambling for all she was worth. As Claire watched her, Jack kissed her nose again. "So. It's all settled. You're coming with me."

I shouldn't, I shouldn't, she told herself. *It's not . . . Not what, Claire van Teiler? Not wise?*

Not *safe?*

She raised her chin. "All right. I'll go." Cocking her head, she planted her hands on her hips. "On one condition."

He melted at her acceptance. "Name it, my love."

"That you dress appropriately for the booth."

He narrowed his eyes suspiciously. "In what?"

"We shall see." She smiled at him.

"Art thou ready?" Claire asked, leaning against the van.

"There's no way I'm coming out," Jack said fiercely. "None."

"Then I'll have to get someone else to help me."

"I'm sorry, but I guess so." He muttered under his breath. "Men were not built for tights."

"Not true," Claire retorted. "And if I have to find someone else, you do too."

"Claire!"

"I mean it, Jack."

"Why are you doing this to me?" he wailed. "I'll be the laughingstock of Julian!"

She didn't know why she was doing it. Deep inside her there was an impishness that only recently had begun to show itself. She felt a mischievous glee at foxing him like this, and it was so delicious, she was loath to suppress it. At the very least, it alleviated the heaviness between them, putting at bay difficult moments and words that would be said when they parted. And at the most, well, she just couldn't wait to see those fantastic thighs silhouetted in black.

"Come out, come out, wherever thou art!" Claire sang. "We can no longer tarry!"

"Tarry, hell! I'm not coming out!"

"Then I shan't either, sir."

"Claire!"

"Jack!"

There was a long pause. "You won't budge on this? I mean, you've got to see it from my point of view. A grown man can't traipse around like this."

" 'Tis my hope that Jessie shall enjoy the benefit," she cooed.

"All right, dammit!" Jack flung open the van door.

She sucked in her breath as he hopped from the van and landed next to her. He was dazzling.

"Oh," she breathed, staring at him. Jack was an Elizabethan courtier come to life. She couldn't believe he was a man of the twentieth century, a cowboy who usually donned worn jeans and simple cotton shirts. She and Amy had pored over portraits of Renaissance men when Amy had decided to try her hand at a male costume, and Jack's chiseled features and magnificent stature matched the period perfectly. She could easily imagine his likeness on a castle wall, the forebear of kings and emperors. She could see him striding from the council chambers, quarreling with Queen Elizabeth herself over a matter of state, serenading a lady over a matter of the heart.

"Oh, you're—you look wonderful."

"I feel damned silly," he grumbled, adjusting his heavy brown velvet cloak. It was lined with leather to give it extra mass, and it accentuated the breadth of his shoulders, making them immense. He towered above her like a great Scotsman driven down into London by the fierce north wind and the command of his liege, Mary, Queen of Scots, to parley with her cousin and mortal enemy, the monarch of England.

"Karen will never let me live it down if she catches me in this," he went on, fussing with his doublet. It was made of luxurious brown and gold embroidered fabric, heavily trimmed with braid, stretching across his chest and nipping his narrow waist. His upper body was a perfect masculine triangle, the frills and fripperies of sixteenth-century taste serving as a stark contrast to his bold manliness.

And his lower body was a paean to that masculinity: short breeches covered his upper thighs, then gave way to black tights that exposed every rivulet of muscle in his legs. The single gold garter encircling his left calf called attention to the well-formed shape of his ankles and feet, prized by Elizabethans.

"By my troth, sir, you are well turned out," Claire murmured, standing on tiptoe as she untied the cloak strings. "Bend down, and I'll drape this correctly."

Cheeks flaming, he obeyed. She positioned one end of the cloak under his right arm and retied the strings across his chest. His arms were clothed in the finest linen, which was stitched in blackwork embroidery with gold thread accents, and she had to force herself not to run her fingers along the bulges of his biceps as she finished her task.

"Oh, Jack," she said. "You look wonderful."

He doffed his black porkpie hat adorned with a white feather plume. "Shucks."

"Now, thou and I must needs speak the proper tongue," she said. "Art ready?"

He hesitated. "Grant me two favors, mistress. The first, a mask."

The imp in her had begun to submerge, and she didn't really want to make him too uncomfortable, so she said, "Done."

He relaxed visibly. "And the second."

"Which is?"

He kissed her long and hard, pressing her lips apart, meeting her tongue with his. His hands gripped her back, pulling her up toward him so that her breasts pushed against her bodice.

She fought at first, mindful of where they were and what they were: a man and a woman irresistibly drawn to each other in the wrong place and time. But Jack wouldn't end the kiss, and wouldn't permit her to do it either, and soon she felt herself answering him. She threw her arms around his neck, felt herself lifted off the ground as he straightened.

"I want you so much, I could carry you into the van right now," he whispered in a rush, his hot breath on her neck. "I could make love to you with a thousand people watching."

"Jack . . ."

He clasped her against his heaving chest, then set her on the ground. "To worketh," he said cheerfully.

Breathless, she nodded. "Aye, milord. To worketh."

"I feel like a kid on a first date," Jack said to his reflection in the rearview mirror of his Lotus.

He was checking his hair for the ten thousandth time. For no reason at all it had chosen tonight to curl every which way, and he couldn't tempt it to do anything else. He had even submitted to the indignity of Karen's ministrations with the blow-dryer, and she'd given up by informing him he looked "pretty good."

"Humph," he'd said, and he said it again now as he swung the car into the compound. He felt a rise of anticipation as he spotted Claire standing beside the corral where Nieve and Pajaro were grazing.

The car rolled to a stop. Pulling on the sleeves of his tux, he climbed out and stopped cold.

This was a new Claire, a Claire he did not know. Gone were the princess dresses and childlike crowns of flowers. In their place stood a polished, sophisticated woman dressed like a Parisienne. Her straight, simple dress of pale gray silk dipped low between her breasts in a series of folds, then clung to her hips and thighs as it plummeted to her feet. The hem was scooped, the sides slit to her knees, emphasizing the erotic overtone of the design. It was a dress made for seduction, for an evening before a fire with a magnum of champagne chilling in a silver bucket and two people with all the time in the world.

Even her hair was different. It was caught up into a sleek chignon from which delicate tendrils escaped to graze her neck. Long, pendulous silver earrings, the only jewelry she wore, caressed the sides of her jaws.

"Claire, how beautiful," he finally said, stunned.

She inclined her head. "You dressed for my century today. I thought I should return the favor."

"You're ahead of my time. The Lord hasn't made women this exquisite yet."

He opened her side of the Lotus and helped her in, his stomach tightening when her dress parted, revealing the tawny hue of her leg and her high heel, a wisp of silver that cradled her small foot. She was dainty and sexy, and his brain rushed forward to the magic hour of midnight, to the delight of taking her dress and shoes off and making love to this new Claire.

He got in and started the engine. They chatted until Jack shot onto the highway, putting the Lotus through its paces like a well-bred horse.

Then he turned to Claire and said, "You must

know how exciting I find you in that dress. Are you teasing me, honey?"

Her neck was incredibly long; he'd never noticed that before. Her head looked small and doelike in comparison, her eyes huge.

"No, Jack. I—I knew what I was doing."

His blood lit on fire. She wanted him! He felt the joy and relief of it boiling through his veins.

"But—" he began, and clamped his mouth shut. He was horribly confused. She ran so cold, and now so hot. What had happened to warm her to him again? He didn't know, but he was afraid of questioning her too closely—she might change her mind.

"Amy and I had a nice afternoon together," she said at last. "I don't think there are any . . . hard feelings between us anymore."

"Over me."

"Yes."

He squeezed her hand. "I'm glad."

Claire relaxed against the seat. "I've never been out with a man in a tux," she said.

"Never? How about your senior prom?"

She shook her head. "I didn't go. Amy had the flu, so I had to stay home."

"What? Couldn't your aunt—"

Touching her finger to his lips, a tender smile curved her lips. "Jack, you don't want to know. Let's enjoy the evening. This is a music benefit, didn't you say?"

"Yes. For the symphony. An early-music quartet is playing."

She clapped her hands in delight, the everyday Claire showing through the chic of the woman beside him. "Oh, how wonderful! How sweet of you to invite me!"

He smiled wryly. His intentions toward this lady were anything but "sweet." In fact, they were deadly serious.

"I've never been in a Lotus before either," she said, touching the dashboard.

He revved the engine. "We've both had new experiences today. I've never been in tights before." Rolling his eyes, he added, "And, with any luck, I never will be again."

She jabbed him playfully. "Oh, come on! You loved all that attention the ladies were giving you. And nobody knew who you were anyway."

He waved a hand. "Ladies pay attention to me anyhow," he said innocently.

"Listen to him! Such modesty."

"You noticed."

"I'm an observant person."

"As am I." And he knew she loved him, he thought. He knew it, dammit! So why wouldn't she stay? Why must she run away from him?

"What do you mean?" Claire asked suspiciously.

He sighed, forcing himself not to say the things that were churning inside him. Don't pressure her, he reminded himself. Don't start a quarrel and ruin the evening.

"Nothing, Claire." He smiled. "Wait until you see the house we're going to. It's got a fantastic view of the ocean."

It did have a fantastic view. Claire was overwhelmed by the beauty of the house, a stately mansion set in the cliffs of La Jolla, San Diego's posh northern suburb. She had thought they were going to a hotel banquet hall, but the private home was large enough to accommodate the two hundred people who had been invited. The exquisite designer gowns of the other women intimidated her at first, and she wondered if she looked out of place. But they gathered around her, demanding to know who her "secret" was. She didn't tell anyone that her little sister had designed and stitched the dress.

The men paid her court as well, and Claire gathered an entourage who followed her across the expanse of Oriental carpets to the Louis XIV love seat, where she found Jack waiting for her with two sparkling crystal glasses of champagne. Beneath the ornate chandeliers the gold in his eyes caught the dancing light, and Claire felt a possessive surge of pride that she was with the handsomest man in the room.

"You're the most beautiful woman here," Jack said, echoing her thoughts as he rose. He waited to be seated until she sank against the silk upholstery. He handed her some champagne and clinked glasses with her. "To you, Claire, who deserves to live in splendor."

She smiled wryly, thinking of her minivan and her cans of beef stew and chili. It would be nice to live in splendor like this.

But this was not reality, she reminded herself. This was a Cinderella fantasy, for one night only. Her life was elsewhere.

"Jack Youngblood! I'm overwhelmed!" cried an elderly woman swathed in a jeweled silk caftan. Ropes of enormous emeralds were looped offhandedly around her neck. "I never thought I'd see you at one of my little soirées! And this is the lady every man in the room is murmuring about!" she added, taking both Claire's hands in hers. "Is this what they're wearing in Paris this season? It's very chic."

"Victorine Schwarzkopf, Claire van Teiler."

"Claire, I'm simply charmed," the woman said warmly. "Any woman who can persuade Jack to come to a benefit is a treasure." She winked at Jack. "And to make a hefty donation, may I tackily add. Thanks to you, we can afford James Levine this season."

"Claire is a musician too," Jack offered. "In fact, she plays the lute."

"Oh, my dear, how fascinating! You'll have to sit in with the quartet after dinner."

Claire blanched. "Oh, no, I couldn't. I—"

"Nonsense, dear. I insist," Victorine said gaily. "*Mes chères*, the prince is here. I do have to make him feel at home. Claire, I'm looking forward to your playing." She bussed Claire on the cheek, gave Jack a hug, and fluttered away.

Claire stared after her, then at Jack.

He raised his brows as he sipped his champagne. "Penny for your thoughts."

She licked her lips. "You're an art patron. This is a part of you I didn't know existed."

"A small part." As they sat back down he drew a finger across the slinky fabric of her dress. "And this is a part of you *I* didn't know existed." He lifted his glass, studying her through a filter of pale champagne. "We have a lot to learn about each other."

And so little time in which to do it, she thought. Lowering her gaze, she ran her finger around the rim of her glass.

A Chinese gong sounded, its mellow tone vibrating through the room.

Jack chuckled. "That's Vickie's dinner bell. Shall we?"

He escorted her past painted antique screens and velvet draperies ornamented with filigreed tie-backs to a huge octagonal room lined with mirrors.

"Oh, my," Claire blurted out, enchanted.

Artificial trees, their limbs sprayed white and studded with twinkling lights, spread their branches over black octagonal tables laden with the dozens of dishes required for a Chinese banquet. Positioned behind each table stood a man or woman dressed in scarlet Mandarin robes.

Claire looked at Jack. "Where do we start?"

The woman behind the nearest table inclined her head. "Please tell me which of the dishes on my table you'd like. I'll be happy to explain them to you."

Jack put his arm around Claire. "Well, sweet, what's your pleasure? What is this?"

"That's *kung pao* chicken, sir. Very spicy."

Grinning, Jack squeezed Claire. "How about it, honey? You're pretty spicy."

"I'd love to try some," she said.

A flashbulb momentarily blinded them. Blinking, Jack rubbed the bridge of his nose and said, "Society pages. That's one of the reasons I don't come to these much."

The waitress had placed a serving of the chicken on two multicolored plates and waited for further orders. "Some saffron rice, perhaps?" she suggested.

"Yes, thank you," Claire replied. She turned to Jack. "What are the other reasons?"

"The Lotus gets rotten mileage. How about these egg rolls?"

The waitress nodded. "They're filled with baby eels, sir."

He made a face. "Yum. Claire?"

"I'll pass, thank you," she said weakly.

"I thought you Elizabethans guzzled down such things."

"Not this Elizabethan."

"The table on your right has pork dishes," the woman told them. "There are three beef tables and one other chicken. Then, of course, we have Peking duck."

"Thanks." Jack picked up Claire's plate as well as his own. "Let's head for the slightly less esoteric."

Claire followed him through the maze of tables. "I just want to know one thing."

"Just one, lady mine?"

"If this benefit is to raise money, how come they spend so much on the food?"

He laughed. "Seems silly, doesn't it? But Victorine is providing the food and drink. No doubt she hired a party planner who came up with the decorations and rented everything. That's very big in the society crowd. But to answer your question, these people have to be tempted by the unusual to come to these things. They have more invitations than they know what to do with. Some of them come to see and be seen."

"Why are we here?"

"To show off. It's not every evening I have such a beautiful woman on my arm."

She bowed her head in acceptance of the compliment. "And do you throw bashes like this?"

He shrugged. "A barbecue now and then. Mexican food. I'm forgiven much because I'm a bachelor."

Out of the corner of her eye she caught the envious glances of the other women. Not for long, she thought, if they have any say.

"My, you're looking glum," Jack said as bits of beef and scallions were daintily arranged on their plates. "Did I say something?"

"Oh, no. I was just thinking."

"Then stop. This is supposed to be fun." He smiled hopefully. "You *are* having fun, aren't you?"

"Yes, of course," she assured him. "Are you?"

"I always have fun when I'm with you." He winked. When she grinned, a huge, happy smile broke across his face. "That's much better. Let's eat now. These plates are so heavy, my wrists are about to break."

Jack found their place cards—their names inscribed on porcelain napkin rings in the shape of lotuses—and pulled out Claire's chair for her. He gave their wine selections to the waiter, then peeked at the other place cards.

"Oh, good. We've got Kim Ferguson and the DeNollys," he said. "Kim's another hoss thief and Patrick and Danielle play in a music consort." He patted her hand. "You'll like them."

She did. She liked it all, from the lobster in oyster sauce to the duck and the Chinese wine to the friendliness of their dinner companions, who obviously adored Jack and were pleased that he had brought her.

"You should get him to come more often," Danielle whispered conspiratorially. "He looks so wonderful in his tux. And your dress is perfect. You must have a very cagey designer."

"Oh, I do," Claire said, enjoying her private joke.

"We're throwing a back-to-school party in three weeks," Danielle went on. "You know, to celebrate our freedom after a summer of the pitter-patter of little feet." She laughed. "Actually, I miss them, but it's so hard to work on our music when they're underfoot all the time. Please come, and bring Jack."

Claire swallowed. "Actually, Danielle, I'd love to, but I won't be—"

"We'll be there," Jack cut in, kissing Claire's cheek.

"Oh, good!" Danielle beamed at the two of them. "Then it's settled."

Danielle turned to talk to her husband and Kim and his date, a beautiful Frenchwoman who swore she'd seen Claire's dress at the Dior salon in Paris. As the four of them chatted, Claire nudged Jack and whispered, "Why'd you tell Danielle that? You know I won't be here."

He smiled pleasantly. "It seemed the easiest thing to do. I'll give your regrets at the party."

"Oh," she said, abashed. It rankled that he would think of going without her.

Well, what did she expect? she asked herself. That he would stop living when she went away? That he would lock himself up on his ranch and live like a hermit?

Of course not. Jack was the most vital, alive man she'd ever met. She could picture him turning down a dozen engagements for every one he accepted, like these other people, and having a marvelous time no matter whether he was at a rodeo or an opera gala. She could see him surrounded by ladies, flirting with them, sleeping with them. . . .

She could see him with Jessie Reynolds.

"Claire? The waiter wants to know if you'd like more wine," Jack said, mercifully interrupting her musing.

"Yes, thank you." She drank it quickly, hoping it would dull the pain.

But the feeling stayed with her even after everyone left the banquet and glided into another room to listen to Renaissance music. Sitting with Jack in silence, his arm around her shoulders as they listened to music Shakespeare had used in his plays, she closed her eyes and felt a cold ache forming around her heart.

And when she played with the quartet her music was tinged with melancholy. A few of the women sniffled into handkerchiefs at the sad ballad she requested, and the bittersweet quality of the lute.

> " 'A king did love a beggar maid,
> So fair a maid was she!
> But too low-born for the lord o' the land,
> Pity little beggar maid,
> Pity mighty king. . . .' "

As Claire played, a tall blonde took her place next to Jack, but he took no notice of her. His features were set, his eyes stormy, and Claire knew he was listening carefully to the words of the ballad. *All my songs have been for you,* she told him through the lute. *We have had sad times and happy ones, and moments that I'll carry with me wherever I go. You've opened me up to the world again, Jack. I'm finally beginning to trust, to expect life to be kind to me. And I'll always be grateful to you for that.* She strummed the lute again. *I'll always love you.*

The song ended, and the Saudi prince led the guests' insistence for another. Claire, still caught in the throes of the ballad, suggested a pavane, for which there were no words. At the conclusion the leader of the quartet shook her hand excitedly and said, "Your playing is superb. Would you consider joining our group?"

"I'm sorry, but that's not possible," she murmured, handing him the lute. "Thank you for asking though."

"Well, if you find it does become possible, give me a call." He handed her a card.

Her first impulse was to hand it back to him, but she thanked him again and slipped it into her purse.

* * *

They left a little after midnight. Jack regarded the fine lines in her face as she looked out the window of the Lotus. She was lost in thought, making perfunctory answers to his questions.

Lord, I hope I've got her wavering, he thought fiercely. *I hope she's as confused as hell.*

He was trying as hard as he could to make it impossible for her to leave him. He was tempting her, painting the loveliest picture possible of life here with him. If she wanted the seclusion of the ranch, so be it. If she wanted glittering society, she would have it. If she wanted him, oh, if only she wanted him . . .

She still hadn't spoken when they reached the ranch. He wasn't sure she was aware that the car had stopped. When he walked around to her side of the Lotus, she started, blinking at him as if she'd just awakened from a long, troubled sleep.

"Come inside," he said, holding out his hand. She began to demur, but he reached forward and firmly took her hand. "Claire, don't run cold on me now. Don't run away."

She took a deep breath. "I won't, Jack. I'm here with you."

But it seemed such an effort for her! He fought back his uneasiness and smiled as if nothing were wrong. "Then come, my love."

Beneath a wide canopy of stars they walked into the house. Jack didn't turn on any of the lights as he led her to his bedroom. Together they moved in darkness. The moon had shifted and no light glimmered through the stained glass in the ceiling.

He undressed in front of her, hoping to arouse her. But in the darkness he couldn't read her face. He heard her gentle breathing, smelled her rose scent, and wondered what she was thinking. How she was feeling.

When he was naked he knelt before her and placed her hands on his bare chest. "Claire, my sweet," he whispered, "won't you let me take off your dress?"

"Yes," she whispered back.

"Don't be afraid of me."

"I—I'm not."

He kissed her, then caught up the folds of shimmering material and lifted them over her head. She was wearing a teddy beneath, and he traced the lacy outline over her breasts. He wanted to tear it off her and make violent, passionate love to her, but he knew she wasn't ready.

"Claire."

"Yes?"

He chuckled throatily. "Nothing. I just love to say your name."

He kissed her shoulder, her upper arm, the crook of her elbow. He felt incredible pressure: He must make her love him enough to stay; he must tempt and beguile her in any way he could; he must be the kind of lover she wanted. . . .

She raised her hands to her hair and began to take out the pins. Coils of hair cascaded down her back like bolts of silk unfurling in the summer breeze. When she was finished she put her hands around his neck and said against his shoulder, "Take me now, Jack. I can't wait."

Bemused, he explored her body. The soft tips of her breasts were taut. Her skin was hot and she was ready for him.

"Oh, my lady," he groaned, laying her back on the mattress.

"Just smelling your cologne," she breathed, "knowing you were naked—oh, Jack, I want you to make love to me."

"Yes, love." He poised himself over her and closed his eyes, savoring the moment.

Then he joined their bodies as one, with a desperation that surprised him. He thrust into her, reveling in her cries of passion, the way she scraped his back with her nails. He strained to please her, worshiping her flesh, tantalizing her, bringing all his masculine powers to bear.

He was so tense that he almost lost his concentration, but it was Claire who brought him back, touching him, caressing him, whispering love words to him. He was astounded, and gratified, and finally the moment of release burst forth from the depths of his being.

Then Claire rocked in his arms, lost in her own explosion, clinging to him and crying his name.

When they quieted, Jack pulled the bedspread over them and fluffed pillows beneath their heads, though Claire preferred to nestle in the crook of his arm.

He dozed. Much later he awoke, aware of a sound in the room.

Claire was standing by a window, holding his tuxedo shirt in both hands, crying. He watched as she ran a hand down the curtain, pressing her head against the glass. Sobbing, she pressed the shirt against her bare breasts.

His heart went out to her. He longed to comfort her. But he closed his eyes and balled his fists at his sides.

Good, he thought, listening to her heartbreaking weeping. Let it hurt too much.

Let it hurt.

Nine

It was still dark when Claire finally gave up on sleeping. Rubbing her eyes, she moved from her place by the window and decided to take a shower. The atmosphere was heavy with sorrow and spent passion, and she couldn't bear to be in it any longer. As she tiptoed through the room the warm summer air carried the scent of apples to her, mixing with the memory of their lovemaking.

Jack was asleep, though tossing fitfully. His lashes were half moons against his cheeks. They stirred like butterfly wings as he frowned in his sleep. Carefully she brushed his tousled hair from his forehead and breathed a kiss on it. She looked down on him with a sad, sweet smile, and a thought rushed into her head: *No matter who else loves you in your lifetime, nobody will love you as much as I.*

"Huunh," Jack mumbled as if somehow he'd heard her. She stepped away, gazing at him in the lightening shadows of a new day. Three more days after this one, and she would be gone.

The bathroom was done in oak and white marble, with rag rugs thrown over white tiles. There were so many plants, it was like a jungle. On the counter was an expensively bound magazine displaying the photographs and vital statistics of various horses around the world for sale, and the addresses of the owners. Rancho Espejo stallions were pictured on several pages.

She found shampoo and soap and thick, fluffy towels. The shower stall itself was made of clear glass, so that she could see all the ferns and palms as she washed. The warm water soothed her eyes, which were puffy from crying and scratchy from lack of sleep.

But nothing, nothing could soothe her heart.

She dried herself off and slipped into Jack's bathrobe, which was yards too big for her. A pine-scented cologne clung to it, and she wrapped the belt tightly, running her hands over the sand-colored velour, snuggling inside. Then she blow-dried her hair.

He was still asleep when she tiptoed back into the bedroom. He looked exhausted, as if he, too, hadn't slept, and she thought about leaving without waking him. But she knew he wouldn't like it, so she stroked his arm and whispered, "Jack. I have to go."

He was awake instantly. He rose on one elbow, running a hand through his hair. "Mmmph." He yawned, then smiled at her. "Good morning, sweetheart."

"Good morning."

He held his arms open to her, and when she didn't respond immediately, he pulled her down beside him. "You look so cute, all bundled up like that. Mmm, smell good too. Did you have a shower?"

She nodded. "Uh, I have to go soon."

He shook his head, yawning again. "Breakfast."

"I don't usually eat—"

He frowned at her. "Breakfast," he insisted. "And anyway, you don't open till ten today. It's Sunday." Nuzzling her with his bristly chin, he asked, "Did you have a good time last night? At the party, I mean?" He grinned.

"Yes. Thanks for inviting me."

"They have those benefits all the time. I could go to one a week if I wanted."

She nodded, not sure why he was telling her that. "But the Lotus gets bad mileage."

"It's fun to drive, though." He scratched first his chest, then hers. "Consuelo's got Sundays off, so you'll have to endure my efforts in the kitchen."

"Oh, I don't want much. Just some toast."

"Nonsense. No wonder you've been losing weight if that's how you eat."

She hugged the robe around her. Was it that obvious? she wondered.

"I'm an observant person," he said, grinning, as if he were answering her unspoken question. "Now, throw me my jeans and I'll whomp you up a real cowboy breakfast."

He did—hash browns and fried eggs, ham, toast, and on top of everything, pancakes. Bare-chested, shoeless, he flipped them with real panache and whistled, "Buffalo Gal, Won't You Come Out Tonight?" as he darted around the kitchen like a short-order cook.

"Grab the juice, won't you, sweetheart?" he called as he set the oak dining room table with straw mats and pottery dishes.

"Yes, sahib." As she opened the refrigerator she felt a pang. This was how it had been when she was little, she remembered, with her father cooking breakfast and her mother assisting him. They had even plastered the fridge with family photos, as Jack had. Since neither one of them had ever taken much interest in domestic matters before Amy's birth, the results of those Sunday mornings had often been catastrophic, to say the least. But amid the chaos, everyone had had a good time, with Amy singing in the playpen and Claire buttering the toast importantly, her father singing folk tunes he'd learned in Czechoslovakia, and her mother laying out hand-embroidered Peruvian napkins.

She could have that again, she thought wonderingly, glancing at the photos of Megan cuddled in Jack's arms. She hadn't lost it forever. Even if Norma hadn't made a family for them, she could still have a new family. She knew the folk songs. She could buy the linens.

She shook the idea away. No. *You couldn't recreate the past. You couldn't go home again.* That was long ago, when she was just a child, before she'd chosen a different kind of life.

"Here we go!" Jack cried, sailing into the dining room with a platter full of pancakes. "Oh, Lord, all this and he cooks too."

Smiling faintly, she filled two glasses with juice and brought them in, setting them down while Jack arranged the silverware at each place.

"Now," he said, rubbing his hands together. He pulled out her chair and waited for her to take the first bite.

"It's good," she told him. He beamed at her and began to eat.

" 'Just some toast.' Right. Please pass the salt, dear."

When she did he kissed her knuckles. "Ah, this is the life, isn't it?"

"Yes, I suppose so." She looked down at her pancakes and chuckled with surprise. He'd formed them into Mickey Mouse shapes, one large circle capped with two smaller ones.

"That's the way Megan likes them." He was drowning his in maple syrup.

"Oh, is she eating solid food already?"

"Nope. But I have an uncle's sixth sense about these things." He lathered some toast with butter and orange marmalade. "I can't wait to take her to Disneyland." Chewing, he leaned his elbows on the table and shook his head. "Karen's going to make me wait until she's *three*. I don't think I can stand it. You may have noticed that patience isn't one of my virtues."

She sipped her coffee. "I think you've been pretty patient lately," she said quietly.

He stopped chewing and put down his toast. His eyes grew soft, questioning. "Do you, Cunky?"

Claire nodded. "Yes. And I'm just sorry that—"

The phone rang. She thought he'd let the machine get it, but he jumped up, saying, " 'Scuse" as he hurried into the kitchen.

"Pop! Yeah. Great. Oh, that's terrific. Yes. Give her a big kiss. See you tonight."

He hung up and came back to the table, looking immensely pleased. "That was my father. They're coming in tonight."

"That's nice."

"So we'll be having one of those barbecues I mentioned," he went on. "You and Amy will come, of course."

She hesitated. "Won't it be a family evening? I mean, I wouldn't want to intrude."

Sighing, he cuffed her gently. "Claire, don't you know by now that you can't possibly intrude?"

"Well, that's very flattering, but—"

"Flattering! I didn't say it to flatter you, for heaven's sake. I said it because—" He exhaled. "So you think I've been patient, eh? That's a laugh."

She touched his arm. "Jack, please, don't let's quarrel."

He nodded and took a drink of coffee. "Sorry."

"I am too," she replied feelingly. "Jack, I really am."

When they regarded each other they looked very sad. Jack gripped her hand and she held on to his fiercely, and in silence they grieved, and tried to comfort each other.

Jack drove Claire back to the compound soon after breakfast, not leaving until she had promised to attend the barbecue. When he returned home he called Karen and she came over right away, putting Megan down for a nap in the nursery while she helped Jack in the kitchen.

"I've tried everything," Jack said glumly as he stirred brown sugar into a pot of baked beans. "Karen, I'm going to lose her."

She turned the faucet off and dried her hands on a dishtowel. "Don't talk like that. I can't believe you're being so pessimistic. You've never given up on anything you wanted."

He tasted the beans and added more sugar. "Claire's not a thing. She's a person."

"You're putting in way too much sugar. Well, I think it was very clever of you to invite Mom and Pop up to meet her. She'll fall in love with our wonderful father and then she won't be able to leave."

"Hah. That's what I thought would happen if she fell in love with *me*." Petulantly he added more sugar.

"You're not as cute as Pop."

"But I'm richer."

Karen looked thoughtful. "I doubt that would matter to a woman like Claire. She really is special."

"I wish she weren't. I wish I'd never met her."

"No, you don't." She peered at his profile. "Do you?"

He turned an anguished face to her. "Oh, Karen." Two tears rolled down his face.

"Poor honey," she soothed, embracing him. He folded over her as if he were limp, wrapping his large arms around her.

"Poor Jack," she crooned, and he began to cry huge, wrenching sobs like the ones that had tormented Claire the night before.

"I'm sorry, I'm sorry," he mumbled, wiping his face.

"Don't be." She rubbed his back. "Boys are allowed to cry nowadays, remember? In fact, it's very in."

"That's not how mah Pappy raised me, gal."

She kissed his wet cheek. "Don't try to joke the pain away, Jack. You know it won't work."

He sighed heavily. "Well, shoot, I don't know what else to do with it."

* * *

Claire was riding. The wind streamed through her hair as Nieve galloped around the outskirts of the fantasy village.

Somehow she felt better. She wasn't sure why, but the breakfast and the prospect of meeting Jack's parents had jolted her more than anything else—perhaps it was the nostalgia of hominess, or the symbolism of meeting a man's family. She wasn't sure.

But she felt calmer as she rode. And the more she spurred the horse on, the better she felt.

She was coming up on a row of garbage barrels filled to overflowing, and she wondered if Lord Petit Sirrah had quarreled with the council over the sanitation facilities. If someone had emptied the trash more often, what would have happened then? Would they have stayed? What then? Would *she* have stayed?

"I'm galloping away," she said aloud. "Riding with the wind. I'm free, as I always dreamed of being. I have my whole life ahead of me. I don't want to settle down now anyway." She laughed shakily. "Sunday breakfasts? I'd go crazy."

You *are* crazy, a voice inside chided her. To ride away from a man like that for a life like this.

"No, for Amy!" she cried. Angrily she gestured for Nieve to swerve around the cans. As the horse complied, a plastic bag piled on top began to sway, then rolled down the pyramid of refuse to be dashed under Nieve's powerful hooves.

Claire heard a sharp squeak. She reined in Nieve and leaped off, running back to the bag.

The bandit eyes of a baby raccoon peered up at her. It chattered at her, struggling to flee, but something held it fast.

"It's okay, sweetie," Claire said. "I won't hurt you."

She dug through the trash, her stomach tightening when she discovered fresh blood on some old newspapers and paper plates.

"Oh, no," she wailed, uncovering the little creature. Its left front paw was covered with blood, and it writhed when she touched it.

"Oh, I'm sorry," she murmured. She hesitated for a moment before lifting it up. It looked healthy but it was so small she doubted it could inflict much damage. It flailed in her grasp, scratching her forearms.

Still determined to rescue it, she held it fast. "I'm so very sorry," she repeated, wincing as its sharp claws pricked her.

When Amy burst into the trailer two hours later, Claire was holding the raccoon, trying to get it to drink some water.

"Yikes!" Amy said. "What happened to him?"

Claire grimaced. "I ran over him."

Amy set down her overnight bag and peered at the frightened animal. "Did you wrap his foot too?"

"No, I saw the vet. He says he should be okay in a few days. I just got the very tip of the paw."

Amy snorted. "When *you* got bashed up, you didn't want me to call the doctor. It's typical that you don't hesitate if anybody—or anything—else gets hurt."

"Just call me Florence Nightingale. How was your night?"

Amy picked up her bag. "It was great. I'll really miss the Hawthorns."

"They seem like nice people. How's the professor's head?"

"All better. They are nice people. Smart too. You know he went to school at Oxford?"

"Wow, classy."

Eyes shining, Amy smiled. "Yeah, and—"

"That must have been expensive," Claire said at

the same time. "I can't believe how high college tuition is. How does anybody afford it?"

Amy slumped. "Yeah, well—"

"What were you going to say, baby? I interrupted you."

"Nothing," Amy mumbled, unpacking the bag and storing her meager belongings.

Claire frowned. "Amy, don't be cross. I didn't mean to interrupt you."

"I know!" Amy shouted. She rubbed her forehead. "I'm sorry, Cunky. I have a headache. I'm going outside."

The door banged shut behind Amy. Claire looked after her, bewildered. "What did I do?" she asked the raccoon.

The animal chattered at her, fighting her.

"Please, I'm just trying to help," she told him, exasperated. "I want to take care of you, okay?"

Not understanding, the raccoon struggled, scraping her already raw arms.

"Ouch!" she cried. "Okay, time for the cage."

She put him in the large wire cage the vet had lent her and secured the latch. The raccoon looked distinctly unhappy, trying to stand on its hind feet, batting at the wire mesh.

"Just till you can take care of yourself," she explained. Sighing, she dabbed some antiseptic on her scratches. Good thing she'd had a tetanus shot last spring. Then she pushed open the van door—or tried to. Somehow it had gotten stuck when Amy slammed it.

She grappled with the handle for a few minutes, then began to pound on the door. "Hey!" she cried. "Amy, let me out!"

But Amy was gone. And Claire was locked in.

Amy avoided Claire during most of the day, once her sister was freed. At first Claire wasn't sure she was deliberately keeping her distance, because they were so busy that there wasn't much opportunity to talk anyway. But even in the moments they had to themselves Amy would avert her gaze and find something to do on the opposite side of the booth.

She was still close-lipped when they shut down for the day and went into the van to dress for the barbecue. And when Jack came to pick them up in the station wagon, Amy sat in the back and stared out the window.

Jack raised his eyes questioningly, but Claire only shrugged, adjusting the beaded belt cinched tightly at the waist of her blue gauze skirt. She also wore a new ribboned peasant blouse Amy had made her, hoping her sister would take it as a gesture of good will. But Amy hadn't even commented on it.

"We used to talk," she told Jack as they climbed out of the car and Amy walked ahead. "We never had any secrets."

"People change."

Claire sighed. "But Amy and I are so close."

He put an arm around her. "I'm sure things will work out." He furrowed his brow as he opened the front door for her. "Is she upset about leaving?"

"She told me she couldn't wait to get out of here."

"Mmm. That doesn't sound like the little sis I know. She's generally so sunny." He held up a finger. "What about poor Davey? He's been moping around too."

"Davey's been forgotten. All she can talk about—when she'll talk—is your friends the Hawthorns. They've been to England, you know."

He smiled. "Ah, yes, your home in the life before."

"Where's that son of mine?" boomed a bass voice from the living room. Heavy boots padded on the rug, then echoed on the wooden floor.

A huge man with salt-and-pepper hair, a weathered, tanned face, and eyes as blue and clear as Claire's poked his head around the corner. He was dressed in a white western shirt and a bolo tie, beige slacks, and boots. When he saw Claire his face broke into a radiant smile.

"Claire, I presume?" he said, walking toward her.

She extended her hand, but he would have none of it, embracing her in a bear hug as he kissed her on the cheek. "Mighty glad to meet you."

"Hi, Pop," Jack said dryly. "I'm glad to see you too."

The man gave Jack an absent pat. "Oh, well, you're just my boy. But this lady here is, well . . ." He made an apologetic grimace at his son as if he'd said too much.

"I'm glad to meet you, Mr. Youngblood," Claire said, a bit overwhelmed by the warmth of his greeting. Now she knew where Jack got his charm.

"Mr. Youngblood's my daddy," Jack's father retorted with good-natured gruffness. "Call me OJ. Everybody does."

They headed back toward the living room.

"It stands for orange juice," Jack told Claire. "Pop had a theory once. . . ." He began to laugh.

"Watch it, young'un. Don't go telling tales on a defenseless old man." He threw an arm around Claire. From the size of his muscles, she judged he was anything but defenseless. "My son's not one for keeping family secrets," he said enigmatically. His eyes crinkled and he cocked his head at her. "You're very pretty," he said. "Your sister resembles you quite a bit, but there are some differences."

"Claire's got your eyes, Pop," Jack said, chuckling. OJ nodded. "Now, the reason they call him OJ—"

"Jack William, you're not too old to whomp if you step out of line."

"—is because after he read about vitamin C—you remember, when all the hoopla about it first came out? He fed all the cows—"

"Look, Claire!" Amy cried from a leather sofa covered with a bright Mexican serape. "Jack's mom sewed Megan a cowgirl suit!"

She held up the baby, resplendent in a red-and white checked shirt, matching bandanna, and tin blue jeans covered with fringed red corduroy chaps Megan gurgled at Jack, kicking her legs when h crossed the room and hoisted her into the air.

"Little Megan Oakley," he crooned, patting he bottom. He made a face. "Fastest diaper-wetter in th West!"

"Ha-ha, Jack, you know the rule," Karen said She lounged beside Amy and Tom on the sofa. On he right sat a lovely middle-aged woman wearing a Mexi can wedding dress and huaraches. Her eyes were a dark as Karen's, and it was with Jack's smile that sh greeted Claire.

"What's the rule?" Amy asked.

"Last one to hold her changes her," Karen said chortling.

Jack looked huffy. "Not that I mind one bit. Com on, Megan. Time for new didies."

As he left the room the woman said, "Hello. You must be Claire. I'm Ruth, Jack and Karen's mother."

"She even made Karen's wedding dress," Amy piped up.

Claire laughed. "How'd you find all this out? You were only in here a minute before I was."

Amy fluttered her lashes. "I work fast."

Gone was the sulking Amy, and in her place the effervescent sister Claire knew—or thought she did Amy was once again the glittering crystal, throwing off her troubles and shining brightly, charming everyone in the room.

And I'm a crystal, too, Claire thought as she shook hands with Ruth. *I thought I lived in shadow but the sun came into my life and freed me. And these are the people who brought him into the world.*

"I'm so glad to meet you," Claire said feelingly. "Jack's told me a lot about you."

"Likewise," OJ boomed.

"Hush," said Jack's mother.

"Would anybody like a drink?" Karen asked, rising. "Jack and I froze a few pitchers of margaritas."

"Goody," Amy trilled, and was instantly quelled by Claire's pointed look. "I mean, I think I'd like a Coke, please."

"Oh, let the girl have one," OJ insisted. "After all, we're only family." He winked at Claire. "You don't mind, do you?"

Claire relented. "I suppose not."

"I mostly just lick the salt off anyway," Amy said.

"Okay, one for everybody then?" Karen rose.

"I'll help you," Claire offered, following Karen out.

"Me too," Amy announced. She trailed after them.

They were almost out of earshot when OJ said, "Damn, that boy's got taste. She's almost as pretty as you, Ruth."

Amy tugged on Claire's blouse. "I think they think you're going to marry Jack," she whispered.

Claire stared at her. "What?"

"Are you?" Amy's voice sounded strained, odd.

"Of course not. We're leaving in three days."

"Oh." Nodding, she fell silent.

Claire stopped in the doorway of the kitchen, preventing Amy from entering. "What's wrong, baby?" she asked. "Are you angry with me because I'm *not* marrying Jack?"

Amy frowned and looked at the floor. "Why would I be? That doesn't make any sense."

"You're happy with the way things are, aren't you? I mean, we've planned our itinerary for the next six months. And I thought, well, maybe we could save up a little at a time and get to England somehow."

She expected Amy to be jubilant, but her sister only sighed and said, "At the rate we're going, that'll take years."

"It might, but we'll still do it. That is, if you still want to."

Amy laughed brightly. "Of course I do, Cunky. We've talked about this for*ever*. I remember how anxious you were last year, waiting for me to graduate so we could get going." She grew serious. "How you worked at that awful job you hated so much so you could support me. And all the times you stood up to Aunt Norma when she threatened to take me away." She squeezed Claire's hand. "It's time for you to have some fun. And me too," she added hastily. "I'm sorry I've been in a bad mood lately. I'll try to do better."

Claire touched Amy's shiny yellow hair. "Oh, baby, you can be how ever you like. I guess my insecurity's been showing lately. I thought you were mad at me for something." For Jack, she added wordlessly.

They walked into the kitchen, where Karen was busily edging seven glasses with salt. "I never did get to tell you about the party," Claire said. "Everybody wanted to know who made my dress. They thought I bought it in Paris!"

Amy preened. "Of course!"

"You're really an excellent seamstress," Karen commented, sloshing frothy, icy margaritas into the glasses. "Those costumes of yours are museum-quality."

"Maybe we should charge more," Claire mused.

"I certainly think so," Karen responded. "Too bad you're on the road so much. I'll bet you could make a fortune selling to stores."

"We could do that anyway," Claire said excitedly. "We could do it all through the mails, Amy! We know our route for the next six months. We could hit the stores in each town, show them samples, and do the clothes at night in camp. Then we could get to England in no time!"

Amy surprised her again. Instead of wildly applauding, she flashed her a smile that didn't reach her eyes and said, "That sounds great!" in a voice totally lacking in enthusiasm.

"Of course, we don't have to if you don't want to," Claire said uncertainly.

Amy shrugged. "Let's talk about it later, okay? Let's just enjoy the party."

"Okay." Claire was bewildered. The strain between them had returned, and she had no idea why. What had she said? What had she done? And why wouldn't Amy just tell her?

"Hah! You lose again, OJ!" Amy shouted triumphantly. She slammed down her Ping-Pong paddle and took a sip of her second margarita.

OJ rolled his eyes and turned to Claire, who was sitting with Jack on a porch swing. Everyone had adjourned from the dining room to the backyard, which was a grown-up's playground, complete with pool—where Tom was swimming laps—Jacuzzi, volleyball net, Ping-Pong table, and a lawn for croquet. In all seriousness, Jack had also installed a tetherball, a gigantic swingset, and a three-room Victorian playhouse from Neiman-Marcus for Megan "a little later on."

"Do you want to play again?" Amy demanded of OJ.

The man was still looking at Claire. "Where'd you find this kid?"

"In a briar patch," Claire responded with the resigned but loving tone so often adopted by parents.

"Cunky!" Amy wailed. She waved her paddle. "Who'll take me on? Are you all chicken?"

"I will!" Karen called. She handed Megan to Ruth. "Mom, will you? I'm going to salvage the family honor."

"Make it a foursome, Ruth," OJ said. "Give Jack the sprout and come bail me out."

"Yes, dear." Ruth walked over to the swing and handed Megan to Jack. "Remember the year we bought our first Ping-Pong set?" she asked, chuckling. "Karen couldn't be bothered. She spent all summer in her room reading teen magazines and listening to records."

"And stuffing her bra," Jack added, chuckling.

"That's the summer Dayton Cook bought the Chevy station wagon."

Ruth tsk-tsked at him. "The things a brother remembers are not the same things a mother remembers." She smiled at Claire. "Wait until he has his own, eh?"

"Ruth!" OJ bellowed.

"Coming, OJ!"

"Would you like to hold Megan?" Jack asked, settling the cooing baby into Claire's arms before she had a chance to answer. "Humph, 'wait till he has his own.' Megan's over here so much, she practically *is* mine."

Megan blinked at Claire, flailing tiny fists. "They say it's different though. Amy's like my daughter, but deep down I know she isn't."

Jack muttered something she couldn't catch. "How's that again?" she asked.

"Nothing, nothing," he assured her. Settling his arm around her, he tickled Megan's nose and said, "Let's watch the game and keep them honest. Karen likes to cheat."

"I'm sure she doesn't!" Claire said.

"Heck, we all do. We're a very competitive family."

"But a very loving one," Claire noted.

"The Waltons, that's us. Just call me Jack-boy."

"Oh, you."

They watched together, Jack standing up to make calls on close shots that the players argued over. Amy was laughing with the others, shaking her paddle when the point went against her side, promising OJ she was going to "whomp him." Megan dozed in Claire's arms, making sucking noises with her tiny shell-pink lips, and birds whistled in the trees. It was a perfect summer evening. A family evening.

At one point Jack touched her cheek and said, "You look so sad. Penny for your thoughts."

Claire stirred, realizing she'd been lost in reverie. "Oh, I was just thinking how much of this Amy missed."

He regarded her until she squirmed. "Is there something you want to say?" she asked with an edge to her voice.

He paused. "I was just thinking, sweetheart, how much of this *you* missed."

"Oh, no," she said quickly. "When I was little we did things like this."

Jack's eyes were kind and loving. "Claire, your parents made you shoulder a lot of their responsibility. You missed a lot."

"Not really. Amy's the one who—"

"Amy's having a great time. She's not dwelling on the past."

A rush of anger flashed through her. "Well, thanks a lot!"

Megan began to cry. "I didn't mean to insult you, honey," he said. "I was just trying to point out that—"

Claire moved Megan to her shoulder, patting her. The baby quieted. "Well, stop trying. You always want to fix me! There's nothing wrong with me, Jack."

"I wasn't trying to fix you, Claire. I just wanted . . . I want . . ."

"Hah!" Amy yodeled. "We won! Claire, we are the champions of the world!"

"Congratulations," Claire called, waving.

"They're back up," Jack said mournfully.

Claire looked at him. "What are?"

"The barriers you build around yourself. You've shut me out."

She felt as if he'd slapped her. Did she really seem so cold, so heartless? "Well, maybe it's just as well," she retorted defensively.

Jack stood up. "Yes, you're right. It's probably for the best." He stepped off the porch. "Hey, anybody up for another game?"

OJ stretched. "Here, take over for your old man, young'un."

"Doesn't Claire want to play?" Ruth asked.

"Nope," Jack snapped. "She's content to be a spectator."

Ten

The evening ended on a vague note. Claire wasn't sure if Jack would continue to see her, and his terse farewell as he dropped them off at the camp sounded final and bitter.

"Gosh, who bit him?" Amy asked as they watched Jack slam the station wagon into reverse and fishtail down the road.

"He's moody, isn't he?"

"I think he's upset about something. He's usually good-natured." Amy opened the van door. "It would be fun to have a brother, wouldn't it? He could have all kinds of cute friends and—eek!"

"What?" Claire tried to peer around her. "What's the matter?"

"Oh, Cunky, that stupid raccoon!" Amy darted into the van and lunged toward a corner. "Come back, you little rat!"

Claire stepped inside. "Oh, no!"

Clothes, flowers, and ribbons were strewn from one end of the van to the other. A bag of lavender had been torn open and the fragrant buds heaped on the floor. Costly fabrics were covered with spilled coffee and ketchup. And in the center of it all, chattering as if it were laughing, bobbed the raccoon.

"You little gremlin!" Claire shouted, trying to grab it. "Shame on you!"

It was still injured enough to make it slow, so after a few attempts Claire managed to capture it. It tried to bite her as it struggled in her arms, and Amy whacked its bottom.

"Claire, throw him outside!" she cried.

But Claire was focused on the animal, gripping its paws in her fists. "Bad!" she said. "Stop that! How'd he get out of the cage? Amy, open the hatch. I'll put him back in."

Amy tugged on the rear end of the raccoon. "Claire, are you crazy? He'll just get out again. We have to let him go."

"Ouch!" Sharp claws dug into Claire's forearm. "Amy, we can't do that. He's hurt."

"He's a wild animal."

"But he needs care."

Amy brushed past her and opened the van door. "He seems to be doing pretty well, I'd say." She softened. "Cunky, there's a time to hold on and a time to let go. It's not right to hang on to him. He'll do better without us."

"Will he?" Claire asked plaintively.

"He'll just be in the way. He has to live his own way, and we have to live ours."

Claire sighed. "But he needs us. We can't just abandon him."

"We're not abandoning him." Amy's shoulders sagged. "For heaven's sake, Claire, stop smothering him!"

Claire's lips parted in surprise and hurt. "Is that what you think I'm doing? I'm just trying to take care of him."

Amy was quiet for a moment. "Sometimes you tend to overdo it," she said hesitantly. "You're not responsible for everybody, you know."

"Now you sound like Jack," Claire answered.

"Do I?"

"But I guess you're right," Claire murmured,

avoiding Amy's question. "The vet said to watch him for a day or so, then let him go."

"So we're not doing anything wrong," Amy added emphatically. "Nature will heal him."

"Okay, you win." Claire carried the raccoon to the doorway and set it down outside. In a flash it scampered away. "It's not even limping. It really didn't need my help."

"At first it did," Amy reminded her. "But not now." She made a theatrical gesture. "A wonderful life lesson for us all, milady."

Claire nodded slowly. "Aye, milady, 'tis that." She shut the van door.

To Claire's relief Jack rode over the next day at twilight and invited them both to another family dinner at his house. They went, but for Claire the evening was a strain. Jack was friendly and pleasant without being intimate, and they never had a moment to themselves to discuss their relationship.

She had no idea what he was thinking or feeling. She assumed he was angry with her, but she wasn't sure anymore. His eyes, which usually darkened like thunderclouds when his temper rose, remained clear and placid.

And when she overheard him telling Karen he might "have a few things to talk over with Jessie," she began to believe it was over between them. He had taken her at her word: she was leaving, and he had to get on with his life. He had written her off.

She was just about to tell him that she and Amy had to go home when OJ slapped Ruth on the knee and said, "Well, woman, time to hit the hay, don't you think?"

"Yeah, man." She smiled at Claire. "We're leaving for Tucson early tomorrow morning. I'm so glad we got a chance to meet you and your sister."

"I am too, Mrs. Youngblood," Claire replied sincerely.

Jack's mother wagged a finger at her. "Remember, call me Ruth. I hope we'll see you again soon."

Claire nodded politely, assuming Ruth Youngblood had forgotten that she and Amy were also due to leave Julian.

Everyone began the ritual of saying their good-byes. Amy hugged Jack's mother and said, "Thanks for the sewing tips. I'm going to make some baby bonnets to sell in our booth."

Claire was about to comment that that was a clever idea when OJ gestured for her to follow him into the kitchen. As she followed him she saw Jack frown in their direction, then turn his attention to his mother when she asked him to smile for a photograph.

When they reached the kitchen OJ leaned against the counter and said, "You know you're breaking my son's heart, don't you?"

Claire's mouth dropped open. "I—I—"

"He's man enough to speak for himself, I know, but I just had to say something. That boy is suffering, and if you have any doubts, *any*, about if you're doing the right thing by leaving, I wish you'd reconsider."

She crossed her arms. "OJ, I—"

He held up a hand. "No need to explain to me. It's between you and Jack." He smiled and patted her shoulder. "And your heart. But by God, girl, I'd be proud to call you daughter."

He left the kitchen without looking back. Claire stared after him, reeling.

Then Amy bounded in, saying, "Karen and Tom are going to give us a lift home, Cunk. Let's go!"

She and Amy joined in the good-byes, Claire saying a hoarse good night to Jack and following the others to the car. Then Jack's sister and borther-in-law dropped them off, and she and Amy went to bed.

Claire prayed for sleep, but none came. And then it was the morning of their last full day in Julian.

* * *

The day dragged by. Jack thought it would never end. At precisely five, when the fair closed, he sent Karen, as planned, to pick up Amy to spend the night at the Hawthorns. Then he showered, changed into fresh jeans and a red and white rugby shirt, and told Davey Bohanon to saddle Thunder.

Jack's heart was hammering in his chest. He'd never been so frightened—nor so determined—in his life.

He spurred Thunder. The horse flew over orchard walls as he cut the space between Jack and Claire by half, then half again. The hours that had stretched like twilight shadows compressed into nerve-racking minutes, then seconds, then anxious ripples up and down Jack's spine.

For Claire, for Claire, for Claire, rumbled the stallion's hoofbeats, like the massive ticking of a clock.

Forever, forever, forever . . .

A million things could go wrong, a million words misspoken. This was Jack's last chance.

For Claire.

He found her carrying a wicker basket of silken squares toward the van. She was wearing a costume he'd never seen before, of hunter's green and white, with small accents of scarlet set in the sleeves and bodice. Her shining hair had been captured by a gold snood that glittered in the sunlight, and the heat of the day reflected the rosy glow of ripe Julian apples in her cheeks and lips.

Oh, be my lady, my lady fair, he cried to her silently, as, hearing the hoofbeats, she stopped walking and looked in his direction. Her eyes were two huge blue worlds, lands he longed to explore and conquer. The glow spread over her face into a blush, making her look vulnerable and shy, and he yearned to comfort and protect her, to make her life beautiful and joyous.

Oh, be my lady, my wife. . . .

"Hi," she said, speaking first.

"God gi'good den." His voice was low, his passion suppressed.

" 'Tis a good den."

When he didn't say anything more she set down the wicker basket and opened the van door, then hefted the basket inside. The vehicle was brimming with boxes and piles of pillows and sachets. Everything was packed in anticipation of leaving. The fair was over, the last galliard danced, the last tankard lifted, the fantasy faded.

"Was it just a fantasy?" Jack asked aloud, his eyes boring into her. She was beautiful, unattainable. His hands clenched the reins. "Tell me, Claire, was it?"

"What?" With a puzzled frown she shut the door. "What do you mean?"

"All packed?" He leaned forward on the pommel of the saddle. She nodded. "Good."

Now was the time to act, to risk the ultimate rejection in his life. Now was the time to dare to do what he might never do again, but what generations of men before him had dared.

Before Claire realized what he was doing he wrapped his arm beneath her shoulders and swept her onto Thunder behind him. Then he flicked the reins and Thunder began to gallop out of the camp.

"What are you doing?" she cried, half-falling in her surprise. But Jack's hand clamped around her waist, molding her against his back as he let the jet-black stallion have his head.

Thunder's hooves struck the earth with powerful force as he carried Claire farther and farther away from the compound. The charger tore through the forest, branches whipping his chest, as if he understood the urgency of his master's mission. He leaped over fallen logs, whinnied as he crested a hill.

"Jack, what are you doing?" Claire demanded again, clinging to him in fear.

He didn't answer. Like a man possessed, he

urged the horse on, fingers digging into Claire's flesh as he held her.

"Jack!" she cried. "Please!"

It was twilight. The sun dappled the tree trunks and gilded Thunder's hooves with bronze. Yet time had stopped for Jack as he rode madly through the wood, wondering if he had done the right thing, wishing he could foretell the outcome of the course he had laid. Feeling Claire's warm, moving body behind him, his heart filled with both purpose and uncertainty, he marveled at the dying sun because it seemed to hover forever just above the horizon. Was this the twilight of a day, he wondered, or of their love?

They reached the ranch. Jack had given everyone the night off. There were no hands in the stable yard, no cowboys currying stallions in the stables, no sounds of cooking in the kitchen. As Thunder slowed to a walk there was only the clopping of his hooves on the soft earth and an occasional trill of birdsong.

"Jack, what—"

He dismounted, then pulled her down into his arms, carrying her toward the house.

"I'm kidnapping you," he said, opening the front door.

"You can't do that!" Obviously nonplused, she struggled in his arms.

His answer was a grim smile. "I'm going to keep you here all night, Claire, and I'm going to make love to you. All night. Until you realize how much you love me and stay here with me." His eyes flashed. "Until you agree to marry me."

Her lips parted. "M-marry—"

"Are you surprised? Didn't you know that was what I wanted?" Gazing at her, he stopped on the stair. "Does that make a difference to you, love?"

She didn't answer. Jack tightened his grip on her and continued up the stairs.

"I want to marry you, Claire. I want to be your

husband, build a life together here on the ranch. I want to be the father of your children."

"I—I—"

He set his jaw, unaware of her fearful reaction, her stunned surprise. "Amy can live with us, for goodness' sake. I don't mind. I like her. You don't have to sacrifice one of us for the other." He frowned at her silence. "You don't have to, Claire!"

"I do! I do!" she cried. A tear spilled down her cheek. "I do have to!"

"No. If you loved me enough, you'd see how wrong you are. And I'm going to make you see that, darling."

At the top of the stairs he turned right, walking in the opposite direction from his bedroom. He stomped down a corridor she'd never seen before, then stopped before a door and pushed it open with his boot.

"Oh, Jack," Claire breathed. "Jack, did you do this?"

"For you."

He carried her into a perfectly decorated Tudor-style bedroom, complete with a dark carved bed and a chandelier of pewter. A timeworn tapestry covered the wall behind the bed, and on the others hung formal oil portraits of the sort she and Amy cherished.

"Tonight we'll make love in your century," he said softly, laying her on the bed. Hangings of burgundy velvet cloaked the two of them in semi-darkness, softening the intensity that tightened Jack's features. "We'll make love through all the centuries. If you were born before, Claire, then I was too. I was brought into the world to love you. Always."

She tried to smile. "Such airy talk from an earthy cowboy."

"Earth and air. And you and I are fire and water. I'm burning for you, my love. So hot, I'm feverish."

He kissed her, filling her soul with his fever, immersing her in his fire. The soft skin of his lips scorched her mouth, her eyelids, even the ends of her hair.

"No, no," she said, gasping, trying to avert her head. "You'll only make it more difficult for me—"

"Damn you, I'm going to make it impossible," he muttered, holding her face between his hands. He kissed her again, his tongue piercing her mouth. She cried out against the invasion and his fingers clamped hard on her shoulder, forcing her to lie still.

He ended the kiss. His chest was heaving. "Say it. Say you don't love me, Claire."

Her mouth worked, but no words came out. Jack leaned into her, studying her eyes. "Say you want to leave me."

"Why are you doing this?" she whispered. "Why are you hurting me like this?"

He closed his eyes. "Oh, Claire, how often I've wanted to ask the same thing of you. So many times you asked me to stay away, and then it was you who came to me. I've seen the way you look at me, as if you were starving, and then I've watched you move away from me as if I were poison."

"I'm sorry."

"You're in love with me. I know you are, dammit! How long will you put your life on hold for Amy?"

She sucked in her breath. Jack gripped her shoulders and shook her. "Answer me! How long?"

"Jack, please!"

"How long?"

"It's not just Amy!" she cried. "It's not just her! I—I—" She burst into tears.

"Oh, baby, Claire, I'm sorry," Jack murmured as he raised her to a sitting position and cradled her in his arms. "I didn't mean to frighten you. I'm sorry."

He rocked her as she wept. "I'm so afraid to love you," she whispered. "Everyone I love—"

"Dies."

She nodded her head against his chest. "And then I'm left alone to face the world."

"But the world is a good place," he murmured against her hair, stroking her back. "There are people everywhere who want to help you and care for you. If something ever happened to me, my mom and pop and Karen would be there for you. And your Amy. And all the other hundreds of people who will love you if only you'll let them."

"Oh, Jack." More tears fell. "I can't stop crying. I . . ." She paused for a moment, felt a loosening in her heart. "I feel so sad."

"When have you allowed yourself to feel anything?" he accused gently. "Haven't you always kept everything bottled up inside, so you could be strong for Amy?"

Her lips parted. "I never mourned for my parents," she said wonderingly.

"Nor for yourself."

"No. I never have."

He kissed her forehead. "What were their names?"

"Richard and Diana."

"So." He settled himself on the bed, leaning against the headboard and pulling her up beside him. Then he clasped her hand in his and laid it against his heart.

"Richard and Diana," he said aloud, "we're letting you go, both of us. Claire and Amy have me, now, and all my family, and there's no more room for all the sorrow your daughter's been carrying around on your account. But she will always love you." He pressed Claire's hand against his cheek. "And I will always love her."

A tear welled in the corner of his eye as he looked into Claire's face. "I will love you, and cherish you, and honor you all the days of my life. And the next life, and the next," he added, smiling tenderly.

"Jack, I'm frightened," she said softly.

"We're standing on a bridge," he told her, "that spans a deep ravine. If you take my hand, I'll help you cross it."

She slipped her hand into his. "Do you really love me?"

He squeezed her. "Yes, I really do."

"And you really want to marry me?"

The room tilted. Jack's heart beat wildly. "Oh, yes, my darling, more than anything."

She took a deep breath. "And Amy can stay here?" She began to wilt. "Oh, Jack, I can't."

"Yes, yes, you can. Everything will work out. Just trust life a little more, love. Trust me."

She picked up his hand and held it so that his fingers spanned her breasts. "Make love to me, Jack. Please."

His panic subsided. He hadn't lost her. "Oh, my darling, there's nothing I'd rather do."

He unlaced her gown and drew it away from her, his chest tightening at the sight of her beauty. Then she stared up at him with light in her eyes, gathering his shirt over his head and snaking his jeans down his legs.

They caressed each other's bodies, exploring as if they'd never made love before. For Claire it was the most freeing, joyous experience of her life. She felt utterly at peace as she touched his hard body, claiming the flesh of her beloved. The fear and hurt had vanished completely, leaving a euphoria so heady, Claire felt drunk with it. Giggling, she embraced him again and again, kissing him everywhere, knowing she would always love him, and that he would always love her. Knowing that, accepting it, expressing it in the act of making love.

When their bodies joined, Jack whispered, "Hello, my wife," and together they rode the crest of the future, of long, golden years filled with adventure, discovery, and delight.

Afterward they lay quietly, Jack tracing imaginary hearts on Claire's stomach. "We didn't use anything," he said. "How will you feel if we just started our family?"

Her answer was to bury her head against his chest and weep.

"Darling, what's wrong?" Jack demanded, alarmed. "Claire, I'm sorry! I should have realized—"

Smiling through her tears, Claire wiped her eyes and shook her head. "Nothing's wrong, my dearest love. It was just the thought of carrying your child . . ." She took a deep breath. "I think it will be the most important thing I've ever done."

He squeezed her hand, thinking back to the day she had watched the breeding with him. He had thought the same thing.

"I love you, my lady fair," he said hoarsely.

She grinned at him. "Then prove it, milord."

"Again?"

"Again."

The next morning the sunlight woke Claire, and for a moment she panicked, thinking, *Oh, no! We'll miss the caravan!*

Then she relaxed against Jack's arm. Today the fair would leave without them.

She rolled her lower lip between her teeth, glancing out the window to gauge the progress of the sun. Amy would be back soon, and they would have to talk. How would she take this turn of events? She would probably feel betrayed, and hurt and angry.

"It'll be fine," Jack said sleepily, pulling her against him. "She'll understand. You'll see, it'll all work out."

"How'd you know that was what I was thinking about?" Claire murmured.

He chuckled smugly. "Husbands always do." He dangled his fingers over her breasts, brushing the nipples with his nails. "So let's go on over there."

She nodded, catching his hand and kissing it. "Thank you for understanding. I didn't think you did."

"At first I didn't want to. Now I'm glad I do. And please know, sweetheart, that I'll try never to intrude on that special closeness you have with Amy."

Claire nodded, praying Amy would know that too.

* * *

They drove to camp in the station wagon. The village had disappeared. In its place were mazes of trucks and cars as the nomads gathered for the next leg of the journey.

"Amy's probably worried sick," Claire muttered, straining to see her through the window.

"Trust," was all Jack said, and she nodded as she slipped her hand into his.

They drove, weaving their way through the crowded meadow. Claire saw Old Tim heaving a cardboard box filled with shoe samples, and Sir Goodwrench, urging a reluctant Merlin into a camper. Good-bye, good-bye, she told them all. And thank you for giving us safe harbor when we needed it.

"There she is," Jack said, pointing through the windshield. "Barbara and Dick are with her."

Amy, with her back to the car, was embracing Mrs. Hawthorn. Jack tooted the horn and she whirled around. To Claire's surprise tears were streaming down Amy's cheeks.

"Stop," Claire said, and she sprang from the Mercedes before Jack had a chance to comply.

"Amy!" she cried, running to her sister.

"Oh, Cunky!" Amy flung her arms around Claire and wept. "I—don't—want—to—go!" she managed to say between bursts of sobs.

"I don't want to either!" Claire cried.

"I want to go to college—*what?*"

Claire beamed at Amy. "I want to marry Jack!"

Amy's mouth dropped open. She looked over her shoulder at the Hawthorns.

The professor smiled delightedly. "Claire, that's marvelous!"

Mrs. Hawthorn embraced both sisters. "Oh, Claire, we're so happy for you."

"Thank you." She looked at Amy. "I was afraid you'd be disappointed, baby. I thought you were jealous of him."

Amy laughed. "We've both been afraid to be honest. I've been wanting to go to college since before I graduated from Revelle. The Hawthorns have been talking to me about going here, and the more they talked the madder I got because I had to leave—*and you're going to marry Jack!*"

"Yes! I am!"

They laughed together and danced in a circle. "Oh, you're so lucky! I mean, gosh, Jack, you're so darn cute!" She fluttered her lashes as he came up behind Claire and wrapped his arms around her waist. "Cunky, are you going to wear a real wedding dress? Can I help make it?" Amy whooped. "Jack! You're going to be my big brother!" She flung herself into his arms. "Claire, we're going to have a real family again!"

Claire's heart tightened as Amy planted a wet kiss on Jack's cheek, and he answered in kind before he tousled Amy's hair.

"Yes, sweetie, we are," she replied.

"And I'm going to *college*. I know exactly what I'm going to take!" She grinned slyly. "I have the entire course catalogue memorized."

"So *that's* what you've been reading so avidly," Claire said.

"Yeah. I have a whole stash of catalogues. I collected them over the summer."

Claire shook her head. "I was so afraid to tell you about Jack. And it would have made both our lives a lot easier if I had. We almost made two bad mistakes just because we didn't want to hurt each other."

Amy hugged her tightly. "We don't need to be afraid anymore, Cunky. We're both going to have what we want."

Claire stood at the end of the aisle on OJ's arm, watching Amy, exquisite in a Victorian gown of soft pink, move with stately grace down the flower-strewn carpet toward the altar of the little Julian chapel.

Karen, in a moss-green version of the same dress, walked ahead of her with Megan in her arms. She had taken over Megan's honorary position of flower girl, decking the path for her brother's bride with petals from her garden hedge.

Jack, with Tom at his side, waited for Claire beside the minister. Through the layers of her veil she took in his dazzling looks, awed that this wonderful man would soon be her husband. He looked splendid in his dove-gray morning coat, his white shirt crisp against his tanned skin and gold-chased eyes. Claire knew bridegrooms were supposed to be nervous, but Jack's joy filled the church until it almost shimmered in the air.

Lord, thank you, Claire thought, her heart swelling with happiness. For everything, for everyone. For letting her know happiness like this.

Then the strains of a wedding march rose like a chorus. OJ patted her hand and whispered, "Here we go, daughter."

Here we go, down a new and untried path. Claire's eyes misted as the congregation stood and turned to honor her. Her white silk hoop skirt belled below a lacy bodice and tight-fitting sleeves embroidered with tiny pink roses and dotted with seed pearls, each one of which had been applied by Amy's loving hands. Clutching her bouquet of roses and orchids—more gifts from Karen's garden—Claire nodded to OJ and they began to walk.

Jessie Reynolds winked at her, looking truly pleased for the two of them. Danielle and Patrick, Victorine—all Claire's new friends—smiled as she and OJ passed them. Ruth dabbed at her eyes and Amy beamed at her, her small face echoing her sister's radiance and love.

And Jack mouthed the words *I love you* as his father led her down the aisle to his side, to his heart, to a life with him.

Then she stood beside Jack, who caught her

hand in his, and the minister began the celebration of marriage:

"Dearly beloved, we are gathered here . . ."

Oh, yes, my dearly beloved, Claire thought, gathering everyone in the church into her heart. *Jack, my love, here we go.*

Here we go.

THE EDITOR'S CORNER

We have four festive, touching LOVESWEPTs to complement the varied aspects of the glorious holiday season coming up.

First, remember what romance and fun you found in Joan Bramsch's **THE LIGHT SIDE** (LOVESWEPT #81)? And, especially, do you remember Sky's best friend and house mate, that magnificent model, Hooker Jablonski? Well, great news! Joan has given Hooker his very own love story . . . **THE STALLION MAN,** LOVESWEPT #119. And for her modern day Romeo, Hooker, Joan has provided the perfect heroine in Juliet McLane. Juliet's a music teacher and musician . . . and a "most practical lady." And it certainly isn't practical for a woman to fall for her fantasy lover! Hooker must teach the teacher a few lessons about the difference between image and reality . . . and that he most definitely is flesh-and-blood reality! You'll relish this warm romance from talented Joan Bramsch.

How many times I've told you in our Editor's Corner about our great pleasure in finding and presenting a brand new romance writer. That is such a genuine sentiment shared by all of us at LOVESWEPT. So it is with much delight that we publish next month Hertha Schulze's first love story, **BEFORE AND AFTER,** LOVESWEPT #120. And what a debut book this is! Heroine Libby Carstairs is a little pudgy, a little dowdy, and a heck of a brainy Ph.D. student. Hero Blake Faulkner is a very worldly, very successful fashion photographer, and one heck of a man! He makes a reckless wager with a pompous make-up artist that he can turn Libby into a cover girl in just a few short weeks. Mildly insulted, but intrigued, Libby goes along with the bet . . . then she begins to fall for the devastating Blake and the gambol turns serious. We think you're going to adore this thoroughly charming and chuckle-filled Pygmalion-type romance! And what a nifty, heartwarming twist it takes at the end!

TEMPEST, LOVESWEPT #121, marks the return to our list of the much loved Helen Mittermeyer. With her characteristic verve and storytelling force Helen gives us

(continued)

the passionate love story of Sage and Ross Tempest, whose love affair throughout their marriage has been stormy (which may even be putting it mildly). And, as always, you can count on Helen to enhance her romance with the endearing elements, as well as the downright funny ones that make her such a popular author. You'll long remember little Pip and Tad, not just Sage and Ross . . . and one very special, very naughty turkey!

A SUMMER SMILE, LOVESWEPT #122, by Iris Johansen is guaranteed to warm your heart and soul no matter how blustery the day is next month when you read it. Iris brings together two of her wonderfully memorable characters for their own bold, exciting love story. Daniel Seifert—remember Beau's captain in **BLUE VELVET**?— is given a hair-raising assignment to rescue a young woman from terrorists. She is Zilah, whom David took under his wing (**TOUCH THE HORIZON**) and helped to heal. Sparks fly—literally and figuratively—between this unlikely couple as they flee through the desert to safety in Sedikhan. Yet, learning Zilah's tragic secret, Daniel is frozen with fear . . . fear that only **A SUMMER SMILE** can melt. Oh, what a romantic reading experience this is!

All of us at LOVESWEPT wish you the happiest of holiday seasons.

Sincerely,

Carolyn Nichols

Carolyn Nichols
Editor
LOVESWEPT
Bantam Books, Inc.
666 Fifth Avenue
New York, NY 10103

P.S. In case you forgot to send in your questionnaire last month, we're running it again on the next page. We'd really appreciate it if you could take the time and trouble to fill it out and return it to us.

Dear Reader:

As you know, our goal is to give you a "keeper" with every love story we publish. In our view a "keeper" blends the traditional beloved elements of a romance with truly original ingredients of characterization or plot or setting. Breaking new ground can be risky, but it's well worth it when one succeeds. We hope we succeed almost all the time. Now, well on the road to our third anniversary, we would appreciate a progress report from you. Please take a moment to let us know how you think we're doing.

1. Overall the quality of our stories has *improved* ☐
   declined ☐
   remained the same ☐

2. Would you trust us to increase the number of books we publish each month without sacrificing quality? *yes* ☐ *no* ☐

3. How many romances do you buy each month? _______

4. Which romance brands do you regularly read?

   ____

   ____

   ____

   ____

   ____

   ____

   I choose my books by author, not brand name ☐

5. Please list your three favorite authors from other lines:

6. Please list your six favorite LOVESWEPT authors:

7. Would you be interested in buying reprinted editions of your favorite LOVESWEPT authors' romances published in the early months of the line?

8. Is there a special message you have for us? (Attach a page, if necessary.)

With our thanks to you for taking the time and trouble to respond,

Sincerely,

Carolyn Nichols

Carolyn Nichols—for everyone at LOVESWEPT

Valentina—she's a beauty, an enigma, a warm, sensitive woman, a screen idol . . . goddess.

GODDESS

By Margaret Pemberton

There was a sound of laughter, of glasses clinking. A sense of excitement so deep it nearly took her breath away, seized her. With glowing eyes Valentina stepped into the noise and heat of the party.

"Lilli wants to meet you," a girl with a friendly smile said, grabbing hold of Valentina's hand and tugging her into the throng. "I'm Patsy Smythe. Have you met Lilli before?"

"No," Daisy said, avoiding the appreciative touch of a strange male hand.

Patsy grinned. "Just treat her as if she's the Queen of Sheba and you won't go far wrong.

Oh, someone has spilled rum on my skirt. How do you get rum stains out of chiffon?"

Valentina didn't know. Her gaze met Lilli Rainer's. Lilli's eyes were small and piercing, raisin-black in a powdered white face. She had been talking volubly, a long jade cigarette holder stabbing the air to emphasize her remarks. Now she halted, her anecdote forgotten. She had lived and breathed for the camera. Only talkies had defeated her. Her voice held the guttural tones of her native Germany and no amount of elocution lessons had been able to eradicate them. She had retired gracefully, allowing nobody to know of her bitter frustration. On seeing Valentina, she rose imperiously to her feet. No star or starlet from Worldwide Studios had been invited to the party. She did not like to be outshone and the girl before her, with her effortless grace and dark, fathom-deep eyes was doing just that. Everyone had turned in her direction as Patsy Smythe had led her across the room.

Lilli's carmine-painted lips tightened. "This is not a studio party," she said icily. "Admittance is by invitation only."

Valentina smiled. "I've been invited," she said pleasantly. "I came with Bob Kelly."

Lilli sat down slowly and gestured away those surrounding them. The amethyst satin dress Valentina wore was pathetically cheap and yet it looked marvelous on the girl. A spasm of jealousy caught at her aged throat and was gone. It was only the second rate that she could not tolerate. And the girl in front of her was far from second rate. "Do you work at Worldwide?" she asked sharply.

"No."

"Then you ought to," Lilli said tersely, "It's a first-rate studio and it has one of the best directors in town." She drew on her cigarette, inhaling deeply. "Where is Bob going to take you? Warner Brothers? Universal?"

"Not to any one of them," Valentina said composedly, not allowing her inner emotions to show. "Bob doesn't want me to work at the studios."

Lilli blew a wreath of smoke into the air and stared at her. "Then he's a fool," she said tartly. "You belong in front of the cameras. Anyone with half an eye can see that."

Noise rose and ebbed about them. Neither of them heard it.

"I know," Valentina said sharply and with breathtaking candor. "But Bob doesn't. Not yet."

Lilli crushed her cigarette out viciously. "And how long are you going to wait until he wakes up to reality? Whose life are you leading? Yours or his?" She leaned forward, grasping hold of Valentina's wrist, her eyes brilliant. "There are very few, my child, a very tiny few, who can be instantly beloved by the cameras. It's nothing that can be learned. It's something you are born with. It's in here . . ." She stabbed at her head with a lacquered fingernail, "and in here . . ." She slapped her hand across her corseted stomach. "It's *inside* you. It's not actions and gestures, it's something that is innate." She released Valentina's wrist and leaned back in her chair. "And you have it."

Valentina could feel her heart beating in short, sharp strokes. Lilli was telling her what she already knew, and it was almost more than she could bear.

She had to get away. She needed peace and quiet in order to be able to think clearly. To still the unsettling emotions Lilli's words had aroused.

She fought her way from the crowded room into the ornate entrance hall. A chandelier hung brilliantly above her head; the carpet was wine-red, the walls covered in silk. There was a marble telephone stand and a dark, carved wooden chair beside it. She sat down, her legs trembling as if she were on the edge of an abyss. Someone had left cigarettes and a lighter on the telephone table. Clumsily she spilled them from their pack, picking one up, struggling with the lighter.

"Allow me," a deep-timbred voice said from the shadows of the stairs. The lighter clattered to the table, the cigarette dropped from her fingers as she whirled her head round.

He had been sitting on the stairs, just out of range of the chandelier's brilliance. Now he moved, rising to his feet, walking toward her with the athletic ease and sexual negligence of a natural born predator.

She couldn't speak, couldn't move. He withdrew a black Sobrainie from a gold cigarette case, lit it, inhaling deeply and then removed the cigarette from his mouth and set it gently between her lips.

She was shaking. Over the abyss and falling. Falling as Vidal Rakoczi softly murmured her name.

* * *

There was still noise. Laughter and music were still loud in nearby rooms but Valentina was oblivious to it. She was aware of nothing but the dark, magnetic face staring down at her, the eyes pinning her in place, consuming her like dry tinder in a forest fire. She tried to stand, to gather some semblance of dignity, but could do neither. The wine-red of the walls and carpet, the brilliance of the chandelier, all spun around her in a dizzy vortex of light and color and in the center, drawing her like a moth to a flame, were the burning eyes of Vidal Rakoczi. She was suffocating, unable to breathe, to draw air into her lungs. The cigarette fell from her lips, scorching the amethyst satin. Swiftly he swept it from her knees, crushing it beneath his foot.

"Are you hurt?" The depth of feeling in his voice shocked her into mobility.

"I . . . No . . ." Unsteadily she rose to her feet. He made no movement to stand aside, to allow her to pass.

He was so close that she could feel the warmth of his breath on her cheek, smell the indefinable aroma of his maleness.

"Will you excuse me?" she asked, a pulse beating wildly in her throat.

"No." The gravity in his voice held her transfixed. His eyes had narrowed. They were bold and black and blatantly determined. "Now that I have found you again, I shall never excuse you to leave me. Not ever."

She felt herself sway and his hand grasped her arm, steadying her.

"Let's go where we can talk."

"No," she whispered, suddenly terrified as her dreams took on reality. She tried to pull away from him but he held her easily.

"Why not?" A black brow rose questioningly.

The touch of his hand seared her flesh. She could not go with him. To go with him would be to abandon Bob and that was unthinkable. He had done nothing to deserve such disloyalty. He had been kind to her. Kinder than anyone else had ever been. Sobs choked her throat. She loved Bob, but not in the way that he needed her to love him. The day would have come when she would have had to tell him so . . . but it hadn't come, and she couldn't just leave with Rakoczi. Not like this.

"No," she said again, her lips dry, her mouth parched. "Please let me go."

The strong, olive-toned hand tightened on her arm and the earth seemed to tremble beneath her feet. It was as if the very foundations upon which she had built her life since leaving the convent were cracking and crumbling around her. She made one last, valiant attempt to cling to the world that had been her haven.

"I came with Bob Kelly," she said, knowing even as she spoke that her battle was lost. "He will be looking for me."

A slight smile curved the corners of his mouth. "But he won't find you," he said. With devastating assurance he took her hand, and the course of her life changed.

She wasn't aware of leaving the house. She vasn't aware of anything but Vidal Rakoczi's and tightly imprisoning hers as she ran to eep up with his swift stride.

She sat in silence at his side in his car, eace and contentment lost to her forever. Some-ning long dormant had at last been released. A est, a recklessness for life that caused the blood) pound along her veins, and her nerve ends) throb. Like had met like. She had known it ıstinctively the day he had stalked across to er on the studio lot. Now there was no going ack. No acceptance of anything less than life vith the man who was at her side.

The car crowned a dune and he braked and alted. In the moonlight the heaving Pacific vas silk-black, the swelling waves breaking into urging foam on a crescent of firm white sand. 'he night breeze from the sea was salt-laden nd chilly. He took off his dinner jacket and raped it around her shoulders as they slipped nd slid down the dunes to the beach. She tepped out of her high-heeled sandals, raising er face to the breeze.

"It's very beautiful here. And very lonely."

"That's why I come."

They walked down along in silence for a vhile, the Pacific breakers creaming and run-ing up the shoreline only inches from their eet.

"You know what it is I want of you, don't ou?" he asked at last, and a shiver ran down er spine. Whatever it was, she would give it reely. "I want to film you. To see if the lumi-ous quality you posess transfers to the screen."

The moon slid out from behind a bank o
clouds. He had expected lavish thanks; vows o
eternal gratitude; a silly stream of nonsense abou
how she had always wanted to be a movie star
Instead she remained silent, her face strangel
serene. There was an inner stillness to her tha
he found profoundly refreshing. He picked u
a pebble and skimmed it far out into the night
black sea.

"I am a man of instincts," he said, stating
fact that no one who had come into contac
with him would deny. "I believe that you hav
a rare gift, Valentina." Their hands touche
fleetingly and she trembled. "I expect complet
obedience. Absolute discipline."

His brows were pulled close together, hi
silhouetted face that of a Roman emperor accus
tomed to wielding total power. He halted, star
ing down at her. "Do you understand?"

Her head barely reached his shoulder. Sh
turned her face up to his, the sea-breeze fan
ning her hair softly against her cheeks. Th
moonlight accentuated the breath-taking purit
of her cheekbone and jaw line.

"Yes," she said, and at her composure hi
eyes gleamed with amusement.

"Where the devil did you spring from?" h
asked, a smile touching his mouth.

Her eyes sparkled in the darkness as sh
said with steely determination. "Wherever i
was, I'm not going back."

He began to laugh and as he did so sh
stumbled, falling against him. His arms close
around her, steadying her. For a second the
remained motionless and then the laughter fade

from his eyes and he lowered his head, his mouth claiming hers in swift, sure contact.

Nothing had prepared her for Vidal's kiss. Her lips trembled and then parted willingly beneath his. There was sudden shock and an onrush of pleasure as his tongue sought and demanded hers, setting her on fire.

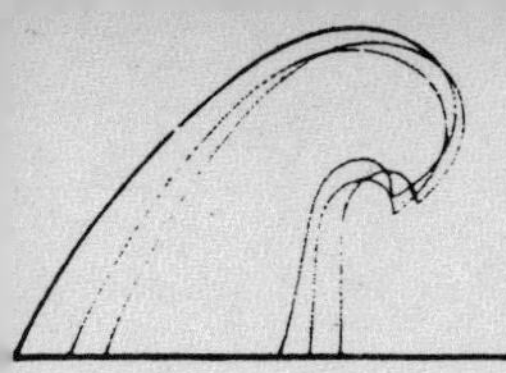